DEEP RUNS THE RIVER

River

A Christian Novel — Book 1

ROBERT HOLLOWAY

ISBN
978-1-960197-68-9 (Paperback)
978-1-960197-69-6 (eBook)

I dedicate this work of fiction to my four children

–Ralph, Lori, Ted, Susan

–who have always been supportive of my varied interests
and endeavors.

Table of Contents

Acknowledgments

I am extremely grateful to Evelyn, my wife of fifty-nine years, for her careful "editor's eye" and computer skills, and her willingness to be interrupted from her activities to assist me and make this the work that it is today.

I am also indebted to Okir Publishing for accepting my manuscript and for the staff's professional suggestions and guidance to bring this novel to publication

Preface

Having taught composition, technical writing, and introduction to literature at the University of Louisiana at Monroe for twenty-three years, I have long wished to be a writer. While I struggled along to find the right words to express my thoughts, I admired those for whom writing seemed to be a special gift. However, aside from some newspaper articles, pieces for some professional publications, unpublished poetry and short stories, I am new at the business of writing. I always found myself waiting for an acceptable idea and theme to develop. Then an early morning dream prompted the idea for this novel. Oh, I can't tell you what the dream was, for I had forgotten it five minutes after I awoke. However, as soon as I was awake enough to ponder, I felt that there was the idea for a novel. Then as I began writing down my thoughts, they just seemed to grow and grow. Except for a few uses of the names of actual places, the work is entirely fictional. It is my hope that, while it is not true, it is truth.

As the theme developed, I confess that it took on a reflection of my own religious beliefs. I make no apology for that because I think they are based upon the solid Truth of the Word of God.

Chapter 1

A New Beginning

"I'm back! Hey, everyone, I'm back. Rusty Jenson is back!" he shouted, but no one was there to hear him. Rusty Jenson is back, back into a world where men set their own alarm clocks, exercise the dignity of work and are compensated with sufficient income to buy bread, where neighbor greets neighbor, and life goes on, aloof from the lowest elements of society. He's back, but no one takes notice or cares. He trudges along the muddy track atop the Mississippi River levee, as it holds back the turbulent waters of the mighty stream. His few possessions are held loosely in a half-filled backpack. Wild flowers bloom along the sloping sides of the bank of soil, leaves burst forth from spring buds, birds flit about the trees chirping, and small animals seem happy as cool mornings replace colder frost. But Rusty lives in a world of loneliness, where he has never been in his twenty-four years. After all the years of clanging sounds, belligerent voices, curses, and shouted orders, he feels the silence, as if a giant vacuum has sucked out all the noises of civilization. In the river a string of barges is being pushed upstream by a struggling tugboat, leaving a plume of turbulence in its wake. But no one welcomes him, knows him, notices him, or shakes his hand. He seeks no destination but a food-laden table and a soft bed. He has no place to call home, and, worse, no one to give him a hug, or even to say "Hello, Rusty, welcome home."

Rusty wonders if his life is not like the turbulent river, which is huge and deep, as it flows through South Louisiana, a long way from where it began as a trickle in Minnesota's Itasca State Park, on its 2,340-mile journey. Millions have walked across its shallow waters at its birthplace. The Mississippi, one of the major rivers in North America, second to only the Missouri in length, drains all or parts of thirty-one U.S. states and two Canadian provinces between the Rocky and Appalachian Mountain Ranges. Along the way to the Gulf of Mexico hundreds of tributaries merge into it, contributing to its vastness. It has changed its course dozens of time, leaving oxbow lakes along the way. Sometimes it flows leisurely, but at other times it floods and rushes along creating whirlpools and treacherous currents and taking with it precious soil from rich farmland and dumping it into the Gulf of Mexico's dead zone. Yes, Rusty thought *my life might be compared to that old river. It too began in a small, insignificant place, but along its path many tributaries deposited their contributions and exerted their influence.* Like the river, which once flowed backward as a result of an earthquake, his life had reversed course often and changed, following the path of least resistance. Or maybe in Rusty Jenson's case the wrong direction had led to an upheaval unlike any other he had ever known. Influences contributed to the changes as his life moved toward its ultimate destination, filling its void with turbulence too.

Reared in a broken home, he lived with his hardworking mother and had a love/hate relationship with his absentee father. He was branded as a troublemaker early in school and dropped out at age sixteen, still in the eighth grade. His peers taught him to smoke, drink, experiment with drugs, and fight, until he became the peer exerting pressure on other young lives. Threatened with juvenile detention unless he went to school or got a job, he found a menial job stacking lumber at a saw mill. Almost no good influences contributed to his life, and neither did he do anything to help himself. No one, not even he, thought he was any good. Now his parents have passed on, relatives have given up on him, for good cause, and friends have forgotten him. But that is the past he has no intention of returning to because his life has taken a new direction. This tall, muscular, blond haired young man sought new work in the same old place where he spent his early years, but with a new nature, a new mission and a new determination. However, he wonders, *what can I do, and who will ever hire me?* He fears that no one will accept him or open their doors to him; nevertheless, he has a new reason to live, a new confidence, a new hope, even assurance like he has never had before. He is free, in more ways than one.

When hunger pangs alert him that it is well past the noon hour, he finds a sheltered place near the river bank under a live oak tree and sits down to eat his cheese and crackers, the only food he has been able to scrounge. After saying thanks he eats in solitude, until suddenly there is animal movement in the underbrush a short distance away. Not knowing whether to run or hide, he waits quietly and watches until a black and white dog comes into sight, a straggler, as wary as he. His dirty, matted hair, and thin body suggest neglect, if not abuse.

"C'mon here, fella," he coaxes, but the dog will come no closer. Rusty wonders what such a dog is doing out here alone, a long way from any house. Does he belong to some area farmer? Has he been abandoned to starve if not taken in by some caring animal lover? But despite his best efforts, Rusty can get no closer than thirty paces to the dog. When he tries to approach, the canine slips back into the brush, but when Rusty backs off, he comes out again to watch him. Rusty feels a kinship: both are alone, hungry, dirty, and without companionship. Finally, giving up on making friends, Rusty shoulders his pack and climbs the levee, thinking he will leave the mutt behind, but the dog surprises him by following at a safe distance. Try as he might to tell the dog to go home, he refuses to leave. *Perhaps he has no home to go to either*, Rusty thought. Since Rusty failed to call the dog to him, he drops a cracker on the path and watches the animal as he grabs it and wolfs it down. As they walk on, more crackers and bits of cheese keep the dog following and gradually drawing nearer. Finally, when night overtakes them, they stop to sleep on the ground and fight the ever present mosquitoes. Before sleep comes, however, Rusty's new friend inches closer, slightly out of arm's reach, but close enough that he can toss him a cracker. They sleep, but the dog is ever alert to any sounds, such as the hooting of an owl, the fish splashing the water, or coyotes yipping in the woods. He makes no sound but seems to be cognizant of all that goes on around him.

Rusty wonders why a border collie, who has all the markings of a purebred, has been abandoned. Perhaps he isn't a good herder and some rancher is not willing to care for him. But for now, at least, Rusty seems to have gained one friend who is sticking closer than a brother, even though Rusty has nothing more to offer him than a bath in the river, a little food, and poor companionship.

When sundown came again, bringing a little relief from the warmth of spring, they found a camp site near the river. But when a large cotton mouth moccasin slithers into the water they decide move on in search of a better place. Finding a suitable one, they "dine" on cheese and crackers, drink from the river, and bed down on the bare ground. The dog comes close enough that Rusty can reach out and almost touch him, and he thinks that maybe in another day he can pet him. Meanwhile the dog is helping to devour the little food they have in a hurry. Rusty lies awake for a long time until finally falling asleep with a voice ringing in his ears: "Go and mend your fences."

His long-standing habit arouses him from sleep long before daylight, and he replenishes the fire, but there is no hot coffee to stimulate him, nor even a pot to make it in, nor a plate of eggs and ham. But the dog and he splurge and eat the last of the meager fare from the pack. Then when it is light enough to see, the friends begin again the trek to nowhere.

Chapter 2

An Unfolding Tragedy

In the upstate town of Winslow members of the Appleby family are facing the most tumultuous time of their lives. In fact, they can't even imagine the changes that have already taken place, and more are yet to come. The family consists of the father, Jim Appleby, an accountant; the mother, Marie, a stay-at-home mom; daughters, Lauren, a senior at the local upscale academy, anticipating her first car for her graduation present; and Cathy, a high school sophomore who is just beginning to pay special attention to the boys. There is also an Appleby son, Ben, the oldest child, who has been labeled the "black sheep" of the family. Dropping out of school at sixteen, still living at home but not working, he does nothing constructive. He sleeps until noon every day, then roams the streets in the 4x4 his dad bought for him to drive to work, which he has never needed for that purpose. When night comes, he can be found in any one of several bars in town. Although he is still below the legal age, because of his family's prominence in town, the police simply look the other way, and his permissive father has long since given up on corralling him. They live comfortably in a roomy two-story brick home in the garden district, and have been very involved in the social life of the town.

Recently Ben has been hospitalized, paralyzed from the neck down as a result of a wild barroom brawl. His progress has been slow, but after weeks of therapy and counseling, he has been discharged to come home. The other family members are well aware of the changes that will come to their family, which they know will affect every one of them; in fact, they have been advised to put him in a nursing home but they have refused so far, determined to take care of their own. A hospital bed has been set up in his room, and facilities adjusted to accommodate his needs. However, for the time being at least, he will be confined to his bed with a catheter and wearing an adult diaper. Once home, a home health nurse will come daily to help bathe and tend to his needs.

When the ambulance brings Ben home and transfers him to his bed, it's obvious that he is filled with hatred and animosity. He doesn't want any help, food, or company, even from his family. Jim arrives home a little after seven, eats his dinner, and at Marie's insistence, goes to check on Ben. But after only a few minutes, he returns to the den and announces to the family, "I just can't stand to go in there. You all are just going to have to see after him."

"Jim, you can't mean that," Marie insists. "He's your son and he needs you."

"I'm sorry, I just can't do it."

Making the adjustments to Ben's presence and attitude is harder than they thought it would be. He is angry at the world. "I would just rather die than be like this," Ben says often. "Why don't you just give me something to just end it all?"

"Oh, no, Ben," Marie begs. "At least you are alive. You still have plenty to live for. You just let us help you."

"I'd rather not see you," he responds, "or anyone else."

Being there to help with Ben took up all of Marie's time. She could no longer go to social events with Jim or give him the special attention he thrived on.

"I can't stand to be in this house," Jim announced one evening. "I think I'm going to move into the club."

"You can't Jim," Marie protested. "Your family needs you. I know that you are having trouble because of Ben, but what about the girls and me? Don't we count for anything? Please don't do anything now. Let's try to work things out." But within a week, Marie got up one morning to find Jim gone. She ran to his closet and found his clothes gone too. He had taken the only good automobile they had and left them to fend for themselves. A month passed without his return; then the postal carrier delivered a certified letter informing her that Jim had filed for a legal separation preliminary to a divorce.

Distraught, Marie telephoned him at work. "Jim, we need you and your support more than ever now. Please don't do this."

"There is no other way, Marie. I'll provide whatever child support I have to and keep Ben on my medical insurance, but I can't maintain two residences, so I've decided to transfer ownership of the house, along with the mortgage, to you."

"Jim, I have always been a stay-at-home mom and been there to take care of you and our children, and now I have Ben, so there is no way I can ever manage on my own and certainly not meet that big mortgage payment."

"You'll have to think of something, Marie. Oh, and please don't call me anymore. You need to get you a lawyer and let him talk with my lawyer."

Soon thereafter, Jim's attorney called and asked her to come by his office to sign the paper work to transfer the title to the property. They agreed on an appointment time, and Marie drove Ben's loud truck, smelling like beer and marijuana, to his office. She was again shocked when told that Jim had borrowed all he could against the house and the mortgage was much more than she had thought. "I can't pay that," she complained. "What am I going to do?"

"I'm afraid I don't know," the attorney responded. "You can always sell the house," he added. "It's a good house, in a good location; however, you need to be aware that there will be little or no equity left for you after the mortgage is settled."

"But I have no other place to live."

"I'm sorry, Mrs. Appleby, but I don't have a solution for you. Now if you'll excuse me I have another appointment. Oh, by the way, I can recommend you a good lawyer for you, if you would like."

"No thanks. Good day," Marie said as she walked out of the office and rushed by the receptionist without a word.

A month passed with Marie looking for a job she could work around her home schedule, which meant a night job when the girls could be home with Ben, but found none. She had some computer skills but no experience in the work place. In addition, no employer could work around her home duties. Then the first payment came due on her house, but she had no money for it. What money Jim provided barely paid for the groceries, utilities, and Ben's medicine. She contacted the bank and informed them that she couldn't make the payment and asked if they could help someway. They assured her that they would work with her for a while, but no more than ninety days. "Well, I have ninety days in this house," Marie spoke to herself. "Should I put it on the market now or wait for foreclosure and ruin my hopes of credit?"

Furthermore, Marie's hopes of being reconciled to Jim faded when she learned that he had been to Cozumel with a young intern from the office. So she sat down with the girls and explained the situation and asked for their suggestions. "Do you mean that we are going to have to move?" Cathy asked. "I've lived in this house all of my life. We will be moving away from our friends, too."

"I'm sorry, darling, but I have no other solution. In fact, I don't even know where we can move too. We'll have to rent, if we can afford that. I'm looking for a job every day, but haven't found anything."

"Maybe I could get a part time job after school or on weekends," Lauren offered.

"Oh I hope you don't have to do that," Marie said. "Let's just hope that the judge will order Jim to pay us enough to live on."

"He'll never do that," Cathy grumbled.

So the next day Marie put a "For Sale by Owner" sign in front of the house, and a few people stopped to inquire about the price and to look at the house, but no one offered to buy it.

"That's too high," they complained. "How much will you reduce it?" Unfortunately, the asking price was only enough to cover the mortgage so she couldn't take less.

At sixty days the bank called to say they would have to begin foreclosure proceedings. Marie knew it would still be a little while before they would be put her out in the streets, but she began looking for a place to rent. To compound the problem, at about the same time, Sarah, the home health nurse, informed her that soon the company could no longer help with Ben because his allotted time was expiring. So Marie faced the fact that she had to go to work at night when the girls could be with Ben, and she could be there in the daytime. Few night jobs were available, but she began looking at every one of them. The only one offered her was a job as a barmaid. Ironically, she didn't even drink, and had never gone to an outright bar. Desperate for some income, however, she took the job.

Fortunately, she had an understanding boss, so her very first night at work she shared with him her need for a place to live. He said, "Let me ask around and I'll get back to you."

It was not a pleasant place to work, but she had been serving family and friends all of my life, so it was something she knew how to do. It didn't take long to learn how to ward off those who thought she was there for more than just a waitress.

A few days later the boss, Smitty, told Marie that he had found a country home that was available to rent. "It's not very large, but it has three bedrooms. It's also a few miles out in the country, but the rent is low. If you are interested I'll take you to the landlord and to see the house tomorrow," he offered.

The house was small. *We will have to dispose of half our furniture or store it,* Marie thought. Since storage is expensive, she decided to sell what she couldn't get in the rent house and maybe get enough money to cover moving expenses. She agreed to rent it, then asked about someone to move them.

Smitty generously offered to rent a truck and call in some favors from a couple of guys who owed him. "When do you want to move? He asked?" She decided to sell the excess furniture and wait until the first of the month to move. She knew the bar was closed on Sunday so she planned to move then.

Marie ran an ad in the paper announcing an "estate sale," and people flocked to the house thinking that they might find some good treasures for little money, and they did. At the end of the day, she found that she could have sold much more if they had not needed it; in fact, she had to put a "not-for-sale" tag on the items she was keeping. It was so troubling for her to part with things that she had been accumulating for years that she had to go into the bathroom to hide her weeping.

As promised, Smitty rented a U-Haul truck and brought three men with him to load and unload the furniture on Sunday, and by the end of the day Marie and the girls had things in pretty good order. Marie had a room to herself; the girls shared a room; and Ben was in his own room. The house had never been updated, and deterioration showed everywhere, but it would have to do for the time being.

However, the more they worked through the day, the angrier Marie became, angry that some young man had created all this havoc, angry at Jim for leaving her in this mess, angry that she had to lose her home, angry about having to sell items of furniture she had been long in collecting, and angry about this little house. She felt like she was back to where she and Jim started twenty-five years before, except she didn't have him now. She had to work nights in a bar, dodging drunks, enduring aching feet, then come home to deal with Ben's hostility.

To cap off all of the other disasters, Sarah, the home health nurse informed Marie that her time was up and she couldn't come any more. Overwhelmed, Marie wondered how they could manage without her help, and asked Sarah as much.

"I don't know, but according to the rules, I can't come anymore. I'm truly sorry. Mrs. Appleby, I know this is hard for you, but it is hard for Ben too. What I think would help him a lot is to get one of those motorized wheel chairs which he can control with his mouth. It would allow him to get out of bed, to spend time with his family, and to even go places." Marie knew she was right, but saw no way they could ever pay for one.

"Perhaps his father would buy it," Sarah suggested.

"Not a chance," Marie asserted. "He is not willing to do anything for Ben. He won't even come to see him. The only thing we get from him is a check for child support."

"Would you mind if I try to find a way to get the chair?"

"But, how could you do that?" Marie inquired.

"Maybe I can find some people to help to raise the funds. Just let me try, Okay?"

"Okay, I guess. I don't like charity, but for Ben I guess I'll have to accept it."

Marie and the girls were sharing Ben's big, loud truck, so they agreed that they needed to trade it for a smaller car or a van that they might be able to load Ben in if the need arose. So the next day she drove the girls to school and began hitting the car lots. Since money was still owed on the truck, she couldn't trade for as new a car as she had hoped. Then when she found a van she could afford, she encountered another problem: the truck was in Ben's name and needed his signature to sell it, an impossibility. So she begged the dealer to allow her to sign Ben's name, and he finally consented. She drove a Nissan van home, and it became their transportation.

Ben was restless all the time and never satisfied with anything: the temperature was not right; the food was not good; the girls made too much noise; he couldn't get up. Most of all, he couldn't stand for his mother and sisters to tend his personal needs, so he took to cursing them and ordering them out of his room. What could they do? They couldn't hit a quadriplegic and they couldn't reason with him. *Just ignore it and put up with it,* Marie thought. Maybe if we will be nice and friendly to him, it will be contagious. But he didn't want pity, kindness, or help. Finally Marie lectured him, "Listen, Ben, we are doing the best we can. Day and night someone is here with you. I'm here during the day and the girls are here while I work at night. I'm working hard for little pay, and Lauren has begun working at McDonalds in the afternoon and weekends just to try to make ends meet. Now if you can manage for yourself you go ahead; otherwise, you will have to depend on us."

At the end of the week, Lauren brought her small paycheck and handed it over to Marie. Even that angered her that she had to take money from her daughter. They were all suffering and being denied their freedom, but she and the girls loved Ben and wanted to care for him at home.

"If I ever see that boy who hurt Ben again, I'm going to hurt him," Marie threatened.

Chapter 3

FAMILY CONNECTIONS

By mid-morning Rusty noticed that the dog's ears stood up at some sound, and a little later he heard it too, the sound of other humans. A truck ground to a halt somewhere and a door slammed in the distance. Rounding the next curve, he spotted the pickup and an old man dressed in overalls putting a jack under the front axle. He has a flat tire so he is trying to change it. When the tire is clear of the ground, he tries to loosen the lug nuts, but to no avail. Apparently frustrated, he leans against the truck. Rusty knew he must be asking, "What will I do now?"

Rusty's "Hello, may I help you?" startled the driver who turned and looked Rusty up and down for what seemed like ten minutes, but it must have been only seconds. Rusty felt like one of the lepers in the Bible must have felt, crying out "Unclean! Unclean!" The man, obviously a farmer, looked like he wanted to tell him to get lost, Rusty thought. Instead, he glared at the flat tire and went into a rant about "them dang impact wrenches tightening bolts too tight. They ought to outlaw every one of 'em."

Without ever introducing himself or smiling, he handed Rusty the 4-way lug wrench, and said, "Alright, you can try it. We'll see how stout you are."

"Maybe I can do it," he responded. And it took all the strength he could muster, but Rusty finally loosened the lugs and removed the wheel.

12

He knew he couldn't have done it if he had not he been in an exercise regime for some time.

The strong young man retrieved the spare tire from the truck bed, mounted it and loaded the flat one into the back of the truck. Then the old fellow opened his mouth, not to thank Rusty but to demand, "What are you doing out here? You don't live around here or belong here."

"No sir, I'm just passing through, walking on the levee. I'm not bothering anything."

"Wal, see that you don't," he grumbled.

Cautiously Rusty took a chance and asked, "Sir, do you have any work I could do? I have very little money and no food left. I'll give you your money's worth, I promise."

"No!" he almost shouted. "Don't you even think about hanging around here. We don't want your kind in these parts. Got too much riffraff now, but to show you my 'preciation for helping me, you and your mutt can get in the back of the truck and I'll go see if the old woman has any scraps she can give you."

Rusty had a hard time coaxing the dog to himself to lift him into the truck but finally succeeded; then "Mr. Anonymous" drove his old truck to near the back door of the farm house and they slide out of the back.

The farmer said, "You jus' stay here, and don't bother nothing and I'll see if I can round up anything for you."

Rusty looked at the house and its surroundings. The screen door on the porch was sagging. Broken limbs from spring's winds littered the yard. The outbuildings were in a sad state of repair. Once upon a time Rusty would have stormed the house and taken food and anything else he wanted, but now he waited calmly until the old man returned with a brown paper bag in one hand and a twelve-gauge shotgun in the other. "Here, take this," he said. "And listen to me, you scumbag. I know what you are and where you've come from. So you take them samwiches and your hound and git off my property, and if you try to steal anything, you'll get a load of this buckshot. If I ever see you around here again I'll call the sheriff and have you arrested for trespassing. Do you understand me?"

Keeping his anger in check, Rusty said, "Yes sir, and I thank you for the food. Tell your wife for me."

Dog and man waited until they were back on the levee and out of gun range before opening the bag to find three baloney sandwiches, no frills, just a slice of meat between two pieces of dry bread. But beggars can't be choosy so they consumed the "feast" with delight and washed it down with river water. As they ate, it occurred to Rusty that he didn't even know the dog's name and guessed that he would have to give him one. He sees the dog looking at him with those big worshipful eyes and says to him, as if he can understand, "I don't know what to call you but you are a real pal, so what if I just call you Pal?" His only answer was a generous tail wag, so Rusty took that as affirmation. "Okay, Pal it is, then."

The land adjacent to the levee soon turned to open pasture and cropland, so he expected to see more farms and people soon, and he hoped to find some better reception than before. Sure enough, they soon spotted a neat farm house with a newly mowed lawn, a sizeable barn, and several equipment sheds. Well-fed cows grazed in the nearby pasture. Flowers were beginning to bloom around the house, and rows of fruit trees were near the barn. It all looked inviting so, warily, Rusty and the dog approached the house and he knocked gently on the front door. A friendly older grey-haired lady answered the door. She wore a neat house dress; unafraid, she opened the door wide and said, "Hello. May I help you?"

"Maybe," he responded. "But I may need to talk with your husband if he is here."

"Yes, he is, but I'm afraid he is not well so you will have to come in to see him. Come on in," she added.

Rusty was embarrassed to walk into a clean house wearing dirty clothes and muddy shoes. He looked like he had been sleeping on the ground, as he had, and had worn the same clothes for days. She led him into the living room where a large man with a warm smile sat in a recliner. "Hello," he greeted him cheerfully. "Come in and take a seat."

Rusty dropped onto the comfortable sofa, and began, "Sir, I hate to bother you, so I'll get right to the point. I'm looking for work."

"Well, what can you do?" he asked.

"Anything you need me to, Sir. If I don't know how, I'll learn how. And I'll be a hard worker."

"Son," the owner began, "it so happens that I do need some help. I'm laid up here with this darn lumbago, and I have some work that I can't get done." He peppered Rusty with questions: "Are you alone? Do you have transportation? Do you live nearby?"

Uh oh, Rusty thought. *Is this going to mean no job?* "To tell you the truth," he responded, "the answer is 'no' to all those questions. I have no place to live, no vehicle, and no family, nothing but a dog."

After a few minutes of silence, the man stuck out his big hand and said, "I'm Albert Hanson, and I'm going to give you a chance. If your work is not satisfactory, you'll have to move on, though. I have a small mobile home out back where some transient workers stay from time to time, so you can sleep there and take your meals with us, and I'll pay you a small salary. Agreed?"

"Yes Sir!" he exclaimed, almost too excited. Just show me where to put my stuff and tell me where to begin work."

"Now hold on," the new boss said. " I don't even know your name."

"Oh, I'm sorry. I'm Rusty Jenson, Mr. Hanson."

"You can begin by calling me Al; everybody calls me that, or worse," he said laughing. "And it's getting late and supper will soon be ready. Besides we don't have a job that can't wait until morning. Mrs. Hanson will show you to the trailer, and when you are showered and freshened up you come on back to the kitchen for supper. Just leave your dog loose in the yard. Mine are in their pen and won't be more of a bother than their bark."

Mrs. Hanson led Rusty to the trailer making small talk about the nice spring weather, and he thanked her at the door. The place was sufficiently furnished and surprisingly clean. Rusty wondered if he had died and gone to heaven. If the food was as good as this place looked, he would work without a salary. Suddenly overwhelmed by his blessings, he fell to his knees and thanked the Lord for His miraculous provisions. Emptying his pack on the bed, Rusty placed his Bible near the sofa where he would see it and remember to read it daily. Then, after a quick shave and shower, he dressed in his other clothes, jeans and a t-shirt, and hurried back to the main house.

Mr. and Mrs. Hanson offered no thanks before their meal, and Rusty didn't want to embarrass them by insisting on it, so he just bowed his head for a silent blessing. They didn't seem to notice, but if they did they didn't say anything. The delicious meal of fried chicken, mashed potatoes, and green beans was topped off with peach pie. Rusty hadn't eaten so well in years and he thanked the Hansons and the Lord profusely.

Rusty asked Al what he had for him to do the next morning, and AL told him that he would find supplies in the barn to begin repairing the corral fence. Then Rusty left to go home. (Home! What a good word.) There, he watched a little television, and went to a comfortable bed in an air conditioned room. He was afraid he might awake in the morning and find that it was all a dream; nevertheless, he got the best night's sleep he'd had in years, and when he awoke the next morning he had some trouble figuring out where he was at first, but when he did he just said, "Thank you, Lord."

He dressed before dawn and headed for the barn where he found the supplies and inspected the broken fence. After sawing some heavy boards to length, he began nailing them up, with the sounds of the hammer echoing across the early morning stillness. An hour later a dinner bell rang at the back of the house and he assumed it was an invitation to breakfast. "What's the matter, boy, can't you sleep?" Al greeted him.

"Yes Sir," he replied. "I'm just used to rising early. I hope I didn't disturb you with my noise."

"No! I'm never disturbed by the sounds of work, especially when someone else is doing it," Al laughed.

"I hope you are hungry," Mrs. Hanson said. "I've prepared plenty, and you'll need a good breakfast"

"Yes, Ma'm, and I thank you for preparing food for me."

For the rest of the week he worked from daylight until dusk and completed most of the work that was needed. In fact, he began to worry that he was working himself out of a job. Saturday evening at supper, Al said, "Rusty the week's work is done and you've done a good job. Tomorrow is Sunday, and we don't work on Sunday, so you'll have the day off." Rusty asked about church and was informed that there was a small church down the road about three miles, but that the Hansons didn't attend church.

Sunday morning breakfast was delayed a little since it wasn't a work day, so when Rusty finished eating he had to rush to make it to church on time; therefore, he excused himself, got his Bible and set out walking to church. As he walked along the gravel road with a spring in his step, he couldn't help wondering if a stranger would be welcomed at the church. He thought if the church folks are anything like the first man he saw, he'd be run off. But when he got there he found a small group of friendly believers led by a godly pastor, with a message from the Bible. He was surprised when the pastor read the text: "If your enemy is hungry, give him food to eat; if he is thirsty, give him water to drink. In doing this you will heap burning coals on his head, and the Lord will reward you" (Proverbs 25:21,22 NIV). Then he spoke on the subject of making friends of your enemies, settling any differences between you. *Had the Lord sent that message just for him?* he wondered, for it reminded him of that admonition, "Son, go and make amends."

After the service and fellowship with the other worshippers, answering questions about where he lived, etc. Rusty started for home, and Pal came out from the shade of a tree and joined him happily. "Hey Pal, so you came to church too, huh?" He was a bit late getting to lunch and explained why, prompting Al to scold him for walking to church and insisted that in the future if he was going to church he should take the farm truck. So, thereafter, he drove to church every Sunday.

Pal was becoming quite skilled at herding the cattle. After only a few lessons, he responded to whistled signals to go left or right, to stop and crouch, and to move forward. He was proving to be a real help in moving the cows from one pasture to another and gathering them for other reasons. Rusty remembered that a border collie is a working dog and needs a job; he loved the work and was a constant companion. If Rusty walked, Pal walked beside him. If he rode the 4-wheeler the dog trotted along with him. And when Rusty got into the truck, pal hopped in the back. In fact, after going with Rusty a few times to check the cows and the fences, Pal took to making that trip by himself. Who knows what he could have done if he had found a problem.

They were into the haying season, so the next week was taken up with cutting the lush grass in the rich river valley meadows; then the following day or two Rusty spent turning it to fluff it up in order to aid the curing process. The fourth day he spent the entire day raking it into rows and bailing it into large rolls, and, finally, on the fifth day he moved them into the large sheds for storage until they would be fed to the cows during the winter months. It was hard work but with the good equipment Al had it was easier than it would have been otherwise.

After work, in the evenings Rusty sat on the front steps and read his Bible every day. One day Al passed by and stopped to chat. "What are you reading?" he asked.

He gladly replied, "I am reading my Bible."

"Oh. That book, huh? Do you believe that stuff?"

"I sure do," Rusty replied.

"I never saw much good in it," Al quipped.

Alert to the possibility to share his faith, Rusty said, "Well, Sir, I can only tell you what it has meant to me. I was worthless, unhappy, and always in trouble. I had no self-esteem and no plans to change. Then I was introduced to the message of the Bible. I learned that we are all sinners, but I felt that I was the worst. I also learned that God loves us sinners and sent His Son to die that we might be saved. Now, to be honest, I didn't see how God could love me. Nobody else did. But this book tells me that Jesus forgives my sins and remembers them against me no more. It says that He makes my life new. Well, I figured I had nothing to lose, so I believed the book and asked Jesus to forgive and save me and I promised to give my life to Him. Now, I can't begin to tell you what a difference it has made. He saved me and is constantly changing my life. Oh, I still experience the effects of my sinful life, but I know that I am no longer condemned; because He loves me, I can now love myself. I wouldn't change it for anything."

Al responded, "Well, that sounds interesting, but I don't know that I could believe in a God I can't see and one who allows so much evil to go on in the world. Besides, I live a good life and, if there is a God, I don't see how He can ever condemn me." Then he abruptly changed the subject. "Tomorrow we will work the cows."

"What does that means?" Rusty asked.

"We will get them all in the corral and catch each of them in that squeeze chute to inspect them, replace lost ear tags, de-worm them, and give them their annual shots to prevent diseases. Then we will release them into the pasture again. We will need some help so I've asked my neighbor to bring his horse and come help us. His name is Snodgrass, and he is an ornery old cuss, but he knows cows and how to handle them."

Chapter 4

BEARING FRUIT

By mid-morning Mr. Snodgrass arrived with his horse in a small trailer. When he got out of the truck he and Rusty recognized each other. He was the man who had a flat tire. He looked at Rusty critically, and grumbled, "What are you doing here?" Then he said to Al, "I can't believe you'd allow this scum on your place. I run him offen my place, and I guess he come down hyar an you took him in. I don't know that I want to work with him. I oughta just go home right now."

Al came to Rusty's defense. "Snodgrass, he's about the best worker I've ever hired. You just watch him when he learns what he is supposed to do and you will see. Besides that he goes to church every Sunday and reads his Bible. That's more than can be said for you and me."

"Ump, that don't mean nothing to me," Snodgrass answered.

Rusty was determined to show "Mr. Uppity" that Pal and he were worth something. In short order the dog and horse working together had the herd in the corral in record time. And the process of putting them one at a time into the chute began. The work went smoothly until the very end, when a large Brahma bull who had evaded the chute all day, was plenty mad and ready for a fight because his herd has been taken away and left him alone. By the hardest, they managed to get him into the squeeze chute and work on him. However, when they were ready to release him they were in for a fight. Al warned them to stay out of his way, and Rusty climbed the corral fence, but Snodgrass stubbornly continued to sit his horse inside the corral as if daring the massive bull. "Here goes," Al shouted as he opened the chute and ran for the fence. Then, the bull was loose but instead of heading for the gate and into the open pasture, the angry bull backed out and charged Snodgrass's horse and drove him against the strong corral fence. Seeing what was happening, Rusty jumped from the fence and Pal came under it. Together, they ran in front of the bull, shouting and drawing his attention, like a rodeo clown, away from the horse and finally managed to distract him and get him out of the gate, but not before Mr. Snodgrass was seriously injured. When Al and Rusty helped him off the horse, it was obvious that he had a broken leg and some other abrasions and bruises. Snodgrass cursed that bull, Rusty, and the dog, blaming them all for his mishap. Rusty just let him blow off steam, but Al tried to persuade him that it was the bull's fault, not theirs. "In fact," he argued, " Rusty and his dog saved you further injuries and possibly saved your life. If you had moved out of the corral as I told you to, this would not have happened."

"Go call 911!" Al ordered Rusty. But Mrs. Hansom had seen the accident and by the time Rusty got to the house she had already made the call.

"The ambulance is on its way," she said. "Now I'll call his wife and let her know what has happened, and tell her that he is on the way to the hospital. Then we will need to go get her and take her there."

When the ambulance arrived and took him to the hospital, Al and Mrs. Hanson drove down the road to the neighbor's farm to get Mrs. Snodgrass and take her to the hospital then wait with her until the doctor came out and said that surgery would be required and that he would need to spend a few days in the hospital, then several weeks recuperating at home.

"What am I going to do?" Mrs. Snodgrass asked. "I don't have anyone to work around the place, and I can't do everything and see after him too."

"We'll help you to manage," Al promised. "You just don't worry about it for now. You have enough on your mind. Would you like us to take you home now?" he asked.

"Oh, no, I want to stay here until after the surgery. Then I'll have to go home to get clothes and the truck, but then I'll come back and stay with him until I can take him home."

"Then would you like us to go get the truck and bring it here?" Al offered. "It's still at our place."

"Yes, that would be nice of you. Thank you," she said. "Then when the surgery is over I can drive home and get my things and him some pajamas."

"Okay, then, we will go do that, and we'll check on you when we get back," Al assured her.

Al and Rusty rode home in silence; there, Rusty unhitched the horse trailer from Snodgrass's truck, and Rusty drove it to the hospital, with Al following. There, Rusty waited in the truck while Al went to check on the patient and give Mrs. Snodgrass the truck keys. Rusty didn't think the grumpy old man would want to see him yet. Al soon returned and reported, "he is out of surgery and stable. He's sleeping right now, but it won't be long before he is awake and grumbling and giving the nurses trouble. Let's go home."

On the way home, Al said, "Rusty, you've caused me some sleepless nights lately."

"How is that, Sir?" Rusty asked.

"Well, I know it isn't your fault, but that stuff you told me about the Bible has kept me awake at night. I toss and turn and think about it until early morning before I can fall asleep. I've spoken with my wife about it, and she says that you are right. I don't know, but I just need to talk with you about it some more. I need you to show me in the Bible where it says those things."

Silently, Rusty said, "Thank you, Lord. Now help me to guide him to You." Then he said to Al, "Well, I'll try. When can we talk about it?"

"I guess we need to do it after supper some night if we can," Al suggested. "The sooner the better."

"Okay. Al, I have something to ask you," Rusty said.

"Okay, what is it?"

"I think, since there are chores to do at the Snodgrass farm and no one to do them, maybe I could go down there after I finish my work at your place every day and tend to their stuff. If I do, however, I will need to borrow the truck. Do you think that would be possible?"

"Of course. But I can't imagine you wanting to take on more work, especially for Snodgrass, after the way he has treated you. What if he objects?"

"Well, we will cross that bridge when we get to it," he said. "Besides he won't know it until he gets home. I'll go today as soon as I finish my work."

"I'll tell you what, Rusty." Al responded, there isn't so much to do here today and I think I can handle it, so you go on as soon as we get home."

Back home, Rusty hitched the trailer to Al's truck and loaded the horse and began his mission of mercy. At the Snodgrass farm he locked the horse in the stall to leave him until he had recovered from the attack. Rusty gave him feed and water and brushed him down. Then he checked on the other livestock to be sure they had food and water. Seeing a chicken yard, he quietly slipped in it to gather the eggs, but since he couldn't get into the house, he decided to take them back to the Hanson's refrigerator and leave them until the Snodgrasses returned. By then it was dark so Rusty headed back to the Hansons.

To his surprise, the Hansons had waited supper for him, and for the first time, Al asked him if he wanted to offer thanks. Rusty thanked God for the Hansons, the food, and for His protection during the day. He also prayed for Mr. Snodgrass to be healed soon and for grace for Mrs. Snodgrass. Silently he was also praying for their meeting after supper because he would need all the help he could get. As they ate he wondered how much of his past he should share. After all, that was a vital part of his transformation and would help in explaining the truth of Christianity. Yet, he hesitated to tell them for fear it might harm their relationship.

As soon as the meal was over, Al said, "All right, go get your Bible and let's talk." Rusty went to the trailer and paused long enough to say a quick prayer for God's help, then returned to the house where he found Al already with a big family Bible out on the table and Mrs. Hanson holding her personal copy she'd had since her teen years. Al said, "Now show me in my mother's old family Bible where it says those things you told me."

"Okay. First," Rusty said, "we need to establish the fact that we are all sinners." He helped him to find the place which says that we "all have sinned and fall short of the glory of God" (Romans 2:23 NIV).

"What does that mean?" Al questioned.

Rusty realized by then that he would have to begin with the most basic information. After all, Al didn't even know the difference between the Old and New Testaments. So he explained that God made the first man and woman – Adam and Eve – perfect and without sin. But they chose to disobey God. "That's sin," he said. Their sin separated them from God. Early on they had fellowshipped with their Creator, but after their disobedience, their sin kept them from Him, and He had to put them out of the Garden of Eden. Remembering Al's comments about being a good man, Rusty said, "Even good men have sinned. None of us is perfect. But the good news is," he continued, "that God still loves us, for while we were still sinners, He sent His Son, Jesus, to earth to die for us and give us the gift of life. However, like any gift, we have to accept it for it to become ours, and we accept it by believing in Jesus and trusting our lives to Him and asking Him to save us. It's called being 'born again.' Even good men have to trust Him to be saved. Once a good man named Nicodemus came to ask Jesus what he must do to enter the Kingdom of God, and Jesus told him, 'You must be born again.' That's what he says to each of us, too."

"Wait a minute," Al said, "how is that possible?"

Rusty chuckled. "You know that is the same question Nicodemus asked, and Jesus explained that from our mother's womb we were born physically, but it's by the Spirit of God that we are born into the spiritual life. I know it's a mystery, but we just have to believe what the Bible says and respond to it by faith." They continued into the night until Rusty finally asked Al if he was ready to invite Jesus into his life.

"Not yet," he responded, "I want to think about this some more for this is some serious stuff, but we will talk again." Mrs. Hanson seemed ready but she said that she would wait for him. After a prayer, they said good night on a positive note, and Rusty went home to pray for the both of them.

The next day was Sunday, and as they had breakfast, Al asked, "Do you think it will be all right if we go to church with you today?"

"Of course," Rusty answered, beaming.

"You don't reckon they will mind us being there, do you? We've never been before. Some of them have tried to get us to go but we refused, and they just seemed to give up on us as a lost cause."

"Definitely not. They will be glad," Rusty assured them.

At church the Hansons seemed uncomfortable and out of place at first, but Pastor Higgins and the congregation made every effort to welcome them and help them to feel at home. The pastor asked Rusty for the first time if he could pray in the service, and he consented. He prayed a simple prayer: "Thank you, God, for this day You have given us, for this church, and for the warm spirit of these believers, and I especially thank you for the kindness of the Hansons who have given me a chance and a job as well as a place to stay. I pray, Lord, for Mr. Snodgrass. Soften his heart and touch his soul with you grace, and I pray for his complete recovery. Thank You, Lord, for saving my soul and giving me new life. Amen." When he had finished Rusty noticed a tear in Al's eye.

God had given Pastor Higgins a message that was just right for the Hansons, and they listened carefully. However, they did not respond to the invitation. That evening when Rusty got to their house for dinner he noticed the Bible was open as if they had been reading it and knew that they would be talking more soon.

In a few days Mr. Snodgrass was sufficiently healed that he was discharged from the hospital. Mrs. Snodgrass told the Hansons that he was really concerned about the farm animals since he thought they hadn't been cared for in days. However, when he came into the yard and looked around, everything seemed to be in good shape. Mrs. Snodgrass still hadn't told her husband that Rusty was tending to his chores. Soon he would know, however.

Later in the day Rusty drove Al's farm truck onto the Snodgrass place, and went about the business of tending to everything. He didn't go to the house, but noticed that Mr. Snodgrass wheeled his chair out to the screened porch and watched him the entire time he was there. He wondered what he was feeling. Snodgrass didn't thank Rusty or even greet him, and Rusty wondered if he was holding his shotgun again.

A short time later Rusty enjoyed the usual delicious meal with the Hansons; then as soon as they were finished, Al said, "Rusty, if you'll tell us how, I think we're ready to trust Jesus and follow Him. I wanted to do it at church Sunday, but I'd rather have you lead me. Can we do it here?"

"Wonderful," Rusty replied. "Yes, you can be saved anywhere." So he took Al's big Bible and showed him two verses of scripture: "For God so loved the world that he gave his one and only Son that whoever believes in him shall not perish but have eternal life" (John 3:16 NIV); "Everyone who calls on the name of the Lord will be saved" (Romans 10:13 NIV). After a moment of meditation, they all got on their knees and Rusty prayed, "Lord, I thank you for dying for us and for saving us. Thank you that this fine couple is coming to trust you. Help them to believe with all their hearts, Lord, and to find the joy of salvation in their lives." Then he asked Al if he would you like to pray and, to Rusty's surprise, he began.

"Lord, you probably don't know me because I've never come to you before. I'm sorry, Lord, that I have rejected You for so long. I see now that I've been denying my sin and trusting in myself instead of you. Forgive me of my sins and save me for I need it, and I'm putting all my trust in you. If you'll have me I'm coming to be yours. Amen."

Then, without prompting, Mrs. Hanson began to pray, "Lord, I also come to receive you, confessing my sin and asking you to save me."

Al just spontaneously burst out, "Thank you, Lord, for saving me. I feel you in my life, and it makes me so happy. Hallelujah!"

Rising from their knees, there were hugs all around, and the Hansons thanked Rusty for leading them to trust the Lord and asked if they could continue their Bible study together. "Of course," Rusty assured them. "Every night after supper we can read and study together." And they did.

A large man stood over Rusty and said, "I told you to go and make amends, and if you don't do it you will sorry. The gang will be after you before you know it."

Frightened, Rusty cried, "No, no, keep them away from me." He made so much noise that he woke himself and it took a few minutes to figure out where he was. What a relief it was when he felt the nice warm bed in a safe place and realized that he had been dreaming. But the "Go and make amends" continued to trouble him.

Chapter 5

A LIVING TESTIMONY

After Rusty had been going to Snodgrass's farm for about a month, one afternoon Snodgrass called to him and ordered him to the porch. Rusty wondered what he wanted but thought surely he appreciated the help Rusty was giving him and wanted to thank him. "You know," he began, "I didn't want you on my place and I still don't, but since you been working here I guess I need to pay you something."

"No Sir, I can't accept your money. You didn't hire me and I'm doing this simply because I want to help you," Rusty declined the offer.

"Wal, I'm getting rid of this cast soon, and then I'll be able to do the chores myself, so you won't need to come anymore. Anyway I guess you are coming because you feel guilty about getting me hurt."

"No, Sir, you know I didn't hurt you or cause you to get hurt. And if you had gotten out of that corral earlier as Al tried to get you too, you wouldn't have been hurt. But I am sorry that you were hurt."

"Let me ask you something," Snodgrass said, in a kinder voice. "Why are you doing this anyway? I've haven't liked you. I ran you off. I cursed you and called you names. Why do you keep coming here?"

"Mr. Snodgrass," Rusty replied, "I'm here in the name of Jesus. Once I was as mean as you want to appear to be, but Jesus came into my life and changed me. Now the Bible tells me to love my neighbor, and to pray for those who persecute me, so I've been praying for you, that you will get well, and trying to show love for you, but also praying that you'll invite Jesus into your heart and be changed."

"Wal, I guess you're wasting your prayers, boy. Ain't no way I'll ever change. I'm too far gone. Besides, I'm happy just as I am."

Rusty replied, "I believe that God does what He promises and He promised that if I will pray He will answer, and if I ask something in His name He will do it. I believe that it is God's will for you to be forgiven and saved. So I'm going to keep on praying for you. I have to go now but I'll see you again tomorrow. Maybe I'll bring my Bible and we can talk about it."

"Forget it," he said, "you little 'do gooder. I hear you done got Hanson going to church, but I reckon I'm too bad for that."

During their Bible study that night, Rusty shared his experience with Snodgrass with the Hansons and asked them to join him in praying for him. "That will certainly be a prayer wast…," Al started saying, but he caught himself and changed it. "If God saved me I believe He can save anyone, even that old cuss. He sure needs it."

The next afternoon Rusty did take his Bible to the Snodgrass farm, but the farmer wasn't on the porch, so he knocked on the door and asked for him, but Mrs. Snodgrass said, "He doesn't want to see anybody. But I'll tell him that you came, and I thank you for your help here. I don't know what I would have done without you, Rusty."

It was two days later before Rusty saw Snodgrass on the porch again and took his Bible in and sat down with him. "What, are you going to preach to me now?" the grumpy old farmer asked.

"No sir, but I want to tell you the best news ever: 'For God so loved the world that He gave His only begotten Son that whosoever believeth in Him shall not perish but have everlasting life.' That's John 3:16."

"Do you really believe that stuff?" Snodgrass asked. "I don't believe in God, that Bible, or your Christianity."

"I'll tell you how much I believe it," Rusty said. "I believe it enough that I trusted my whole life to Jesus. I'm banking my future on it. Let me ask you something. You say you don't believe in God or heaven and hell, and I say that I do believe it. Suppose when we die we discover that I'm wrong, that there is nothing after death. If that is the case, I've lost nothing but a life of misery and sin. It has been replaced with happiness and hope. I have a good life. I would be no worse off if there were no afterlife. But what if you are wrong, and there is a God who will be your Judge, and there is a hell where the unsaved will go forever? What will you lose?"

"That's enough," Snodgrass said: "you need to go now."

"Okay. Good evening, Sir. I'll be praying for you tonight and see you tomorrow." The Hansons and Rusty prayed as never before for Mr. and Mrs. Snodgrass that night, and afterward Rusty had a peace about the situation. Maybe this is "making amends" Rusty thought, but deep in my heart he knew this wasn't all. There was something more he had to do.

For another week he visited with Mr. Snodgrass every day and finally he was allowed to pray in his presence. Then the very next day, Snodgrass said, "Rusty, based on what you've said I think I'm on the way to hell unless I'm changed. Maybe I'm about ready to give this Christian thing a try. Tomorrow I want you to come again and maybe I'll do it and see if will do any good."

Knowing that a vital part of growing in faith is helping others to trust Christ, Rusty told the Hansons that he would like them to go with him to the Snodgrasses the next day and share their testimony with them and lead them in praying the sinner's prayer. They seemed frightened by it, but they agreed to do it.

The next day Rusty asked Mrs. Snodgrass to join them all on the porch and he asked Al to tell them what had happened to him. When he finished, to Rusty's surprise, Mrs. Hanson added her testimony also. Then Al led them both in the sinners' prayer. When they raised their heads, Rusty thought he had never seen such a glow on a man's face. Snodgrass hugged him, the Hansons, and his wife, and she burst out, "Thank the Lord. You don't know how long I've prayed for this, Elijah."

"You have?" Elijah Snodgrass asked. "I never knew you believed in God."

"Oh, yes, since I was a little girl. But you've been so opposed to it that I could never talk to you about it. Do you think we can begin going to church now? I would so like to sing the hymns again and hear the Bible preached."

"Sure, we'll go next Sunday and see if they'll let us in."

Al said, "Let us pick you up Sunday and we'll all go together."

That very week Mr. Snodgrass was freed again – from that dreadful cast. And the next Sunday both of them walked the aisle and professed Jesus as their Savior. Two weeks later the Hansons and the Snodgrasses were baptized and welcomed into the membership of the church.

Fall was turning to winter and Rusty could see that there wasn't as much to do around the farm in the winter time, and, in addition, he had learned that Al usually just hired seasonal help, so he thought that it was time for him to move on. When he told Al that he was thinking he should go, Al asked him to stay on. "It's true that I won't need help during the winter, and I can't pay you but you can stay on in the trailer and eat at our table until spring." But Rusty knew there were fences he had to mend elsewhere.

However, a week before he planned to leave, Rusty asked Pastor Higgins if he could share his testimony at church. He knew it would be humiliating but it was something that he felt compelled to do. He thought he might have been dishonest in keeping it from everyone this long. The pastor agreed for the next Sunday and Rusty prepared himself.

When Pastor Higgins presented him to the congregation and told them he would be giving his testimony, he bragged on Rusty, "We've found Rusty Jenson to be a fine Christian. He has been a model among us and I am anxious to hear what he has to say; welcome him." Everyone clapped, but Rusty wondered if the pastor and congregation would still feel the same way when he had finished.

Nervously, Rusty pushed himself to the podium and began: "Before coming here I was a guest on an 18,000-acre plantation down in the bend of the river, called Angola, the Alcatraz of the South." A collective gasp went up from the pews, but he continued. "I wasn't raised in a Christian home. We never went to church. I was mean, and at an early age began drinking and doing drugs, fighting, and getting arrested. Then one night in a barroom brawl another boy was hit with a chair and was hurt so badly that he is now a quadriplegic. I was too drunk to know whether I did it or not, but another young man came forward and told the police that I swung the chair. I was arrested and charged with attempted murder. The courts found me guilty and I was sentenced to seven years of hard labor and shipped to Angola.

"Life there was not easy: Gang activity, beatings, and murder were a common thing among the prisoners. I was one of the lucky er, I mean blessed ones. Of the 6,000 incarcerated there, 90% will die there. I hated others and was hated by them. I knew that if I had been released quickly I would have gone back to my old way of life, only worse than before, a hardened criminal. But one day the assistant chaplain called me to his office and said to me, 'Son, I hear that you are not getting along very well here. You are not working out on any of the jobs you are assigned to and not fitting in with the other prisoners or the guards. You are just making it hard on yourself; you know we have ways of dealing with people like you. But I think I know what's eating at you; you are loaded with guilt and have no hope. The greatest enemy here is the lack of hope. But you are better off than most: you have only seven years or less with good behavior. You can see the light at the end of the tunnel. Eighty percent of the inmates are here with life sentences. I'd like to make a suggestion to you. We have church services here and a Bible College that you can attend and help yourself. You'll get along better here and be better prepared for life outside when you get out if you will take advantage of them. This experience will be what you make it. It can make you worse of make you better. You decide which.' I wasn't interested in going to church, but to relieve the boredom, a week later I attended church for the first time in my life, a prison church. I sat in a congregation of prisoners and heard the gospel preached for the first time in my life, but I didn't know how to believe or what to believe. Later some of the Christian inmates approached me and began sharing their Christian experience with me, and they gave me a Bible, the first I had ever owned. I really began to see that they cared about me, and they convinced me that God loved me. So over the next few weeks I learned how to become a Christian then accepted Christ as my Savior. My life changed immediately. Those saved inmates taught me and soon I enrolled in classes to earn my GED, then a college degree. I spent the next four years learning the Bible and growing in my faith. And I soon became one of those inmates who was helping others to come to know Christ and grow in faith.

"On my fifth anniversary at Angola, the papers came through to discharge me, and the assistant warden called me to his office. 'Hello, Rusty,' he said. 'The reports show a great change in your life since you first arrived here and I've learned why. I've also read the reports about the criminal activity that sent you here. Now I warn when you are released some of your former friends will try to get you back into their habits, and you will need to try hard to avoid the temptations. Of all the prisoners who get out of here, most of them are back in a few months unless they have met the Lord here and been changed as you evidently have. Those don't usually come back, and I don't want to see you here again. Now you go and mend some fences. Good luck to you.' They offered me a ride on the prison bus into Baton Rouge, but I was drawn in another direction and persuaded them to bring me to this side of the river by boat. Guards escorted me down to the river bank where a large oak tree stood with limbs outstretched like a cross. I thought how symbolic; this old tree is like the cross of Jesus. Both represent my entrance into a new life and liberty. The rest is history. I wound up at the Hansons and they trusted me and have been wonderful employers and friends. And you all have accepted me and been a great help to me. Thank you. I guess I have to say I'm thankful for having been in Angola, too. I would really like to stay here, but I have something to do. I have to go back to my hometown and find the man I hurt, Ben Appleby, and try to make amends. So I'm saying goodbye to you. I'll be leaving soon."

As he returned to his seat, the whole congregation rose to their feet and applauded. Then Al Hanson stood and asked, "May I say something? When Rusty came to our place with that border collie, I sensed that there was something different about him. Oh, he was dirty as could be from sleeping on the ground and had mosquito bites all over him. But I saw a man with a good attitude. I needed some help and something just told me to give him a chance. I've never regretted it for one minute; my only regret is that he is leaving. Now, because of him, my wife and I are saved. Thank you Rusty."

When Al sat down, Mr. Elijah Snodgrass stood and said, "I don't know how to talk so well, but I gotta tell you something too. Rusty came to my place first, and I was afraid that he had come from the prison. He politely helped me change a flat tire, then asked for a job. I cursed him and ran him off my place. And I resented the fact that Al hired him, and I blamed him for my broken leg when I was really responsible for it. Then while I was in the hospital, without being asked, he took care of my chores and kept on even after I came home, and he did it without pay. Then when he told me about his Christ, I realized that I had already seen Him in Rusty Jenson. He don't just believe it, he practices it. And because of him, me and my wife are also Christians. I'm so grateful I'm on the way to heaven instead of hell. I judged him wrongly and condemned him when I was not as good as him, and I hope he will forgive me for it. But now I'm happy to say, we are brothers in the Lord now."

By this time, there was hardly a dry eye in the house, and the pastor said, "Thank you, Rusty. We will pray for you as you go home on this important mission. We will miss you, but we understand why you must go. Well, folks, we've already seen and heard the best sermon today, so we will be dismissed."

It seemed to Rusty that everyone in the congregation came to hug him and wish him well. Rusty felt such a relief that he had bared his soul and pledged himself to do it more often, to stop trying to hide his story, for it was a vital part of who he had become.

Chapter 6

GOING HOME

A week later, Rusty packed his few belongings and a sack lunch Mrs. Hanson had prepared for him, and Al drove him to the bus station. Pal had jumped into the truck as they were leaving the farm, so at the station Rusty sat down on the ground and put his arm around Pal and tried to tell him goodbye. The dog looked at him with sad eyes as if he knew that his friend was leaving him. Rusty told him, "You be a good dog, obey your new master and work hard. You will a partner to Al now." He knew that unless they kept Pal from it that he would try to follow the bus, so they locked him in the cab of the truck, and with tears in his eyes Rusty watched his sad face at the window as Al drove away.

It was a long day's ride with all the stops along the way, and as they rode Rusty remembered the story from the Bible of Jacob going home to be reconciled with his brother Esau and how afraid Jacob seemed to be. He felt a kinship to Jacob. He made it home to the North Louisiana town of Winslow late in the afternoon, retrieved his meager luggage from the belly of the bus and walked down the familiar streets. Home is where family and friends are, but Rusty had neither there, so it really wasn't home to him, just the place where he had grown up. Little change had taken place in Winslow, but it looked different to Rusty for he saw it through new eyes. Once he would have looked for a place to break into or to get some drugs or get into some other trouble. The hardware, the drug store, City Café, the pool hall, and the same old bar lined the first block. There was the church in the second block. He'd never been inside, but he knew he soon would and wondered if he would be accepted there. Surely some of the congregation would recognize him as that Jenson delinquent, ex-con. Fathers would not want their sons to associate with him, and mothers wouldn't permit their daughters to date him. They may not even give him a chance to prove himself.

He would attend church, but he knew that he had a greater mission. "Go and mend your fences" was no longer the command of an assistant warden ringing in his ears; it was a divine mandate. He planned to seek out Ben Appleby and apologize and seek his friendship and forgiveness. Whether he gives it or not Rusty knew that he would do everything in his power to improve Ken's life. Rusty searched out the street where Ben had lived with his family in a nice red brick home, but when he arrived there was a new family name on the mailbox. *Surely someone here will know where they are now*, he thought.

He drew from the money he'd saved working at Hanson's and paid for a room at a cheap motel. The clerk, who appeared to be from India, asked for an ID, but nothing else about his past or his business. She wanted only to know how many nights he would stay.

"Just one night," he answered. "I hope to find some more permanent place to live." After all, the money he had would not last long, and he didn't know how long it would be before he found a job. He might be sleeping on the streets soon. After a good night's sleep, he walked to the City Café. Pop Jones was still there, but looking older, a little more stooped when he came to take his order. He said, "Good morning. You look familiar. What's your name?"

"I'm Rusty Jenson," he responded. "I used to live here."

"Jenson, Jenson," Jones murmured. "Can't say I remember that name. My memory is not what it used to be though. But welcome back. You aim to stay long?"

"Yes, I do. I'm looking for a job and a place to stay. If I can find those I'll probably be here for a long time." At 9:00 a.m. he entered the office door to the First Church. A cheerful, middle-age receptionist greeted him with a smile and asked, "How can I help you?"

"I would like to speak with the pastor if he is in."

"O yes, Dr. Williams is in his office. I'll ring him. May I tell him who's calling?"

"I'm Rusty Jenson. I used to live here. You may remember my name."

"No. But I'm kinda new in town." After a moment, she said, "the pastor will see you now. Just go right through that door with the 'Pastor' sign on it."

A grey-haired older gentleman sat behind a cluttered desk, but when Rusty entered the room, he got up and came around the desk and gave him a firm handshake like he was glad to see him. "I'm Ben Williams," he said, "welcome to my office."

"I'm Rusty Jenson," he introduced himself.

"Hello, Rusty. Do you live here?"

"I grew up here, but I've been away for a few years and I just returned. I hope to stay here."

"Well, wonderful," he said. "Say, I have a pot of fresh coffee. Would you like a cup."

"Yes, thank you. That would be good. I'm afraid that I had at the City Café this morning wasn't the best."

"Ah, yes, old Brother Jones keeps it going, but he's slipping some. Cream or sugar?"

"No, thank you. I take it just the way it comes out of the pot."

As they sipped the coffee and chatted a bit, Pastor Williams asked, "How may I help you this morning?"

"I need three things, Sir. I want to know if I will be welcome in your church, first. Second, I need a job, and finally, I need a reasonably priced place to live."

"First, let me say that you will be very welcome at this church. Is there some reason you might think otherwise?"

"Yes Sir. Apparently you don't recognize my name. Of course, I've never been to church here or anywhere else in town. But you may remember the incident when Ben Appleby was injured in a barroom brawl."

"Yes, I do remember something about that, but it has been a while, hasn't it? In fact, I think we helped to raise money to buy him one of those motorized wheelchairs he can control with his mouth. Come to think of it, I haven't heard from him in some time. How long has it been since he was hurt?"

"About six years now. I am the man who was accused of injuring him. I was found guilty of attempted murder and sentenced to seven years of hard labor at Angola. Just a few months ago I was released after just five years, and I've been working on a farm down south this summer. So I didn't know if an ex-con would be accepted here at First Church. But I assure you I'm not the same man I was before. I was saved in prison and attended the Bible College they have there and earned a full four-year degree in Christian studies. I had to get a GED first of course, because I was a high school dropout. I had convinced myself that I was dumb and couldn't learn, but when I graduated college with honors, I gained a new sense of self-esteem. Now, with Jesus in my life, I'm a new man."

"Good. Good. I assure you that I will accept you and I'll do everything I can to lead this congregation to welcome you. Those who remember you and know about your incarceration may be a bit slower, however. We have a very conservative, older congregation so they'll watch for you to prove yourself. I've heard of the program the warden has going and the good work the school is doing. From what I hear, the violence at the prison has been reduced about 75 percent, hasn't it?"

"I believe that's about right."

"Now, about that job, I don't know anyone who is hiring, and I'm sure that it will be more difficult for you to find work because of your record. But I believe that God will provide, and I'll be praying that you find work. As for a place to live, I may have better news. We have an older couple who have a small house behind their house where his mother used to live. Since she passed away, they have rented it out some, but I believe it's vacant at the present time. I think that if you will be up front with them about your situation, they might rent it to you. If you wish, I'll call them and make an appointment for you to see them. Let me write their address down for you. I'm putting it on the back of my card so you'll have my number also."

Handing Rusty the card, the pastor said, "let me call them right now and see when it will be convenient for them to see you. What's the best time for you?" he asked.

"Anytime is fine with me."

He dialed the number and after a moment, said, "Hello, Brother Howie. This is Pastor Williams. Is that little rent house of yours still vacant? Good. I have a young man in my office who is looking for a place, and I wonder if it would be possible for him to see you about it? Two O'clock today? Yes, I'm sure that will be okay with him. His name is Rusty. You have a blessed day, now. And I'll see you Sunday. Goodbye."

"That's wonderful," Rusty said. "Oh, there is one other thing I need to ask you. Do you know where the Applebys are living now?"

"Well, I know about where they live, but, given your history with the family, I'm a little hesitant to give out their address. I don't know enough about what you are going to do or whether they will want you coming around. Sorry."

"Oh, that's okay. I understand completely."

After leaving the church, Rusty went to the shopping center to try to buy some clothes. He still had only the two outfits he'd been wearing for months and they were pretty worn from working in them. At the department store a young man was very helpful in finding him two pairs of pants and shirts, along with socks and a new pair of shoes. He was shocked at how much prices had increased. He dressed in one of the new outfits and the new shoes before leaving the store so he could look presentable to the Howies and while job hunting.

Before the two O'clock appointment, Rusty called on two places looking for work, but neither needed help. When he met the Howies, he liked them immediately. Like Al Hanson, they brought him right into their living room, seated him on the nice sofa and served lemonade. "Say your name is Rusty?" Mr. Howie asked.

"Yes Sir."

"What is your last name?"

"Jenson."

"Jenson. Any relation to the Jensons who used to live here?"

"Yes Sir. Oscar Jenson was my father. Both my mother and father have died in the last few years. My brother and sister moved away, so I have no close relatives in town now," Rusty answered.

"Tell me about yourself, Rusty."

"Okay, Sir. But it's not the best of stories." Then he told him about his experiences, from start to finish. "I'm not sure you'll want me around now that you know, but I assure you I'm a changed man now."

"You're right, I might not," he responded. "But I believe in giving a man a chance. And I believe that if you are a Christian, you are my brother, and I'm not supposed to turn you away. So I think I'll rent you the house if you want it. Let's go look at it."

Howie led him to a furnished house with a living room, bedroom, kitchen and bathroom. A porch stretched across the front of the building. A rocking chair was on it, and he could picture that old woman who had lived there sitting, rocking in the cool of the day, and humming a tune.

The price was reasonable, and all Rusty needed was to buy some groceries and move in. "Thank you, Mr. Howie; I think it's just what I need. May I move in today?"

"Yes, you can. And since you'll be busy getting set up, you can join the missus and me for supper. Tell me where you are working."

"Unfortunately, I don't have a job yet, but I'm looking and trusting the Lord to bless me with one. I learned some skills while in prison that I think I can use now. My favorite is woodworking, so I'm going to check in on that."

He walked to the neighborhood grocery and bought coffee, bread, eggs, bacon, lunch meat, a newspaper, and a few other items. After carrying them home and putting them away, Mr. Howie knocked on the door to announce that supper was ready. He offered a prayer of thanks before the meal and prayed for Rusty to find a good job and to be happy here. A delicious bowl of clam chowder with French bread, followed by apple pie topped with ice cream was filling as well as good. Soon after the meal he thanked the Howies profusely for the place to live and the appetizing supper. Back in his new house, he searched the want ads in the newspaper, but found nothing that seemed promising. However, the next morning he hit the streets seeking a job everywhere he went. Most places were not hiring, and the two that were rejected him when they learned he was an ex-con. Trudging along home, he talked to the Lord and prayed for a miracle.

Days passed with no success. "Can you pass a drug test?" prospective employers asked, and he assured them that it would not be a problem. Next they asked, "Ever been in trouble with the law?" and he had to tell them the truth.

Chapter 7

MAKING AMENDS

Lauren was excited when she graduated because she thought she would get the car her father had promised her, but when she called on him, whom she hadn't seen in months, to ask for a car, he turned her down. "But you promised," she argued to no avail.

"I can't afford to buy you a car now; I'm having to pay too much child support. Ask your mother to buy you one."

"Well, you are not paying nearly enough if you ask me," Lauren responded angrily. "Maybe you could take some of that money you're spending on your new girl friends. And another thing, I want to know why you never come to see Ben. I know it's not pleasant but he is your son and since we are with him 24/7, you could at least come for a visit. If you can't do that, you just forget us all, okay?" She was furious by the time she left his office.

"That's enough, Lauren. You may go now."

Almost every week Ben would ask, "When is Dad coming to see me? I want him to get me out of this hellhole. He can take me to his place and hire someone to care for me."

"I'm sorry," Marie told him, "but I'm afraid he isn't coming. I wish there was something I could do, but it looks like you'll just have to settle for the women in the family."

"That sucks!" Ben shouted.

One day, just as Marie finished feeding Ben his lunch, and before she ate herself, the telephone rang. It was from United Health Supplies informing her that the wheel chair would be delivered the next day and that the company would send a representative to teach Ben how to use the chair, her how to recharge the battery, and how to maintain the device. In addition, he would demonstrate to Marie and the girls how to safely transfer Ben from the bed to the chair and back again. Marie had even forgotten about Sarah's promise to raise money for a chair, thinking it was just idle talk.

Marie could hardly believe her ears, for she had heard nothing from the home health nurse, so she found her card and called. "Sarah, they just called to say that Ben's chair would be delivered tomorrow. How did you get the money?"

Sarah, overjoyed herself, said, "You won't believe it. I asked a gospel quartet to have a benefit concert, and they did. Then the Kiwanis devoted their "Pancake Day" receipts, and First Church took up a special offering. So we got the full amount."

"Thank you so much, Sarah."

"Marie, if it's all right I would like to be there tomorrow when the representative trains you if I can get someone else to fill in for me," the nurse requested.

"Sure," Marie responded. "Please do." As soon as they hung up Marie made a list of all those who helped in order to be able to mail thank you notes to them, especially to Sarah.

One good thing about Lauren's graduation was that she could then drive Cathy and herself to school early in the morning. However, Cathy got out of school at 3:30, three hours before Lauren's shift ended, so she had to ride the school bus home. After work, Lauren rushed home to have dinner with her family every day before Marie had to leave for work herself.

As promised, the wheel chair arrived at 10:00 the next morning, right after Sarah. A nice gentleman, named Cayman, brought it into the house and began showing them everything about it. Ben had said that he didn't want it, but Marie saw him watching carefully as the representative explained all about the chair. Then the time came to move Ben from the bed to the chair. He balked. "I'm afraid you will drop me," he complained.

Cayman calmly asked the ladies to excuse themselves and he talked with Ben, explaining the process in standing him beside the bed and turning him to be seated in the chair. "I promise I'll not drop you," Cayman said.

"You may not, but I don't think my sisters and mother can do it," Ben argued. Listening from the living room, Marie could hear every word of their conversation. She then realized that Ben's biggest problem was fear, fear of the future he faced, fear of dependence, and fear of helplessness.

"Ben, don't you want to get out of this bed, out of this room?" Cayman asked. "Besides, if you aren't moved more your joints are going to freeze up and bedsores will develop on you backside." With a lot of coaxing, Ben finally allowed Cayman to pull his legs off the side of the bed, lift him to a standing position, and swivel him around to lower him into the chair. He then spent an hour showing Ben how to control the chair with his mouth and practice the maneuvers. Although Ben tried not to show it, it was obvious that he was delighted with the chair and its possibilities. Cayman then instructed Marie how to make the transfer and they practiced it, confirming that she could do it, so more and more Ben began to trust her to do it.

With the chair in use and the instructions complete, Sarah told Marie, "I wanted to come today so that if you ever need me I can come and help. Even if I cannot come in an official capacity, I'll come on my own time if you call me." With that promise she excused herself and left.

When Cathy got off the bus, Ben showed her how he could move around, and she teased him: "When you get out of it, I'll play on that thing. You're not the only one who will have wheels."

"No way," Ben actually laughed. "It's mine."

At the little Appleby house, everyone, including Ben, was just seated for dinner when Lauren announced that she was leaving McDonald's for a job at the TLC Nursing Home. "Are you sure that's what you want to do?" Marie asked. "That's hard work and just dealing with a bunch of old people and invalids, helpless people." She had said it without thinking, so she quickly apologized to Ben and explained," I wasn't referring to you." But the damage was done already.

Ben suddenly wheeled away from the table and headed for his room. Too late Marie realized that she had said the wrong thing, so she got up to go to Ben's room to apologize again. "Don't come in here," he demanded, and to prevent it he had rolled the chair against the door. She knew it would be days before things returned to normal again.

Back at the dinner table, Lauren said, "I have something else to tell you;" she whispered so Ben wouldn't hear.

"You mean there's more," Cathy said.

"Yes, I saw someone at work yesterday who told me that Rusty Jenson is back in town."

"What?" Marie demanded. "How did he manage to get out early? I'll bet he escaped."

"I don't think so. They said he got out early for good behavior and that he got religion while he was in prison. He's really changed, he claims."

"Yeah," Marie chimed in, "I'll have to see it to believe it. On the other hand, I don't ever want to see him again. If I do run into him, I'll probably do my best to cripple him as he did Ben."

"Now, Mom," Lauren said.

"Don't 'now Mom' me, I hate him and I always will, and I hope you two do also," she asserted. "Why did he come back here anyway? Nobody in this town should accept him. Where can he find a job? Where is he going to live?"

"Well, I don't know," Lauren continued, "but I hear that he is going all over town looking for a job, and rumor has it that he has even gone to First Church to talk to the pastor."

"Don't you go near him. Do you hear me? If you see him, go the other way. He is nothing but trouble. Has anybody ever been rehabilitated in jail? We probably won't have to worry about him for long because he will be back in jail somewhere."

It was time for her to go to work, so they persuaded Ben to go back to bed while they were all present. With Lauren's help, Marie was able to get Ben into bed, but it wasn't as easy as she thought it would be. "That's not as easy as Cayman made it look," she exclaimed." With Ben safely in bed, she warned the girls to lock the doors and not to answer the door for anyone, certainly not that criminal Jenson. "Yes, Mom, they responded together." Then she rushed off to work, not to return until after midnight.

Chapter 8

TESTED AND TRIED

As Rusty's job search proved fruitless, he decided that the Lord was just putting him to the test to see if his faith would be shaken. But, to be truthful, he was feeling really down, and wondered if he was going to be able to stay in Winslow. Yet this was the place that he felt he must stay if he was going to mend the fences from his broken past. So he continued to pray and look for a job.

As he walked home one evening feeling sorry for himself, a loud 4X4 rumbled up beside him and stopped at the curb. "Hey man," a familiar voice shouted over the loud music coming from the truck. "When'd you get out?" the old friend, Buddy, shouted.

"I've been back in town for a couple of weeks," he answered. Then Jack rolled out of the passenger side and grabbed his hand and shook it vigorously. "Say, old friend, we're glad to see you. Let's go down to Mike's Bar and celebrate. C'mon, get in. We'll have us some beer and look at the girls."

Rusty knew that it was not wise for him to go, but he was so discouraged and these were his old friends. What would it hurt? he thought. So he climbed in the truck and they roared down the street to their old hangout. Willie Nelson whined out "Ain't Going Down on Brokeback Mountain" from the juke box as they entered the dark interior of the bar. When they were seated at a table, Rusty noticed that Buddy went over and whispered to the pretty waitress before joining them at the table. When she came to take their orders, they said, "go ahead, Rusty," and he said, "I'll just have a coke please."

"Aw, c'mon," Jack and Buddy said simultaneously. "We're celebrating. You can't celebrate with coke. Bring us three beers," he ordered.

When the shapely waitress returned and placed a coke and three beers on the table, Rusty noticed that Buddy pointed the girl to him, and he thought, "Uh oh, I'm being set up." She sidled up to him put her arm around his shoulder and rubbed her body against him. "Drink up, handsome," she said, "and we might have a little celebration of our own after work." It had been so long since he had even had a date that she was very tempting. Why not? he wondered. He deserved it. But as he reached for that mug of beer like old times, a verse of scripture came to his mind: "Be happy young man while you are young, and let your heart give you joy in the days of your youth. Follow the ways of your heart, and whatever your eyes see, but know that for all these things God will bring you to judgment" (Ecclesiastes 11:9 NIV).

"Fellas," he said. "I'm glad to see you again, but I want you to know that I'm changed. I've trusted Jesus Christ as my Savior, and my life belongs to Him. I can no longer live like I used to."

"Oh, c'mon," Buddy insisted; "So you are a Christian; that doesn't mean you can't have a little fun and enjoy a beer and a roll in the sack with a sexy woman."

"You're right," Buddy, "but I find fun in different ways now. I know that one beer is not going to hurt, but to me it is just bait to lure me into more. I never want to go back to what I was before. So I'm going to say, 'good evening.' By the way, before I go, there is nothing I would like to see more than you to be saved. So I'm going to be praying for you to be saved."

"Ha! Ha!" they laughed. "You're not a man anymore. You're just a pansy. Ha! Ha! Ha!" Even if it meant the loss of friendship, Rusty walked out without looking back.

At home, he knocked on Mr. Howie's door and asked, "May I speak with you? Sir."

"Sure, anytime," he replied. "Is something wrong?"

"Well, I don't want to do this but I haven't been able to find a job and I don't have enough money to pay the rent for next month, so I guess I'll be moving out in a few days."

"But, where will you live?" he asked.

"I don't know, but I can't pay you."

"I'll tell you what, Rusty," Howie said. "I know that you are trying, so you're going to find work soon. You forget about moving for now, and when you get a job you can begin paying rent again. Tell me again, what kind of job you would like."

"The job I liked best at Angola was in the woodworking shop. But I've been to the construction companies and they won't hire me."

"Rusty, let me see what I can do. My son has a sizeable cabinet shop out on the edge of town on Highway 91. Maybe he can use you. I'll talk to him and let you know something tomorrow. Meanwhile, we're about to have supper, so join us."

The next day was Saturday. Mid-morning Mr. Howie came to Rusty's rented house and knocked on the door. He began, "Rusty, I talked to my son, Clark, and he just might make a place for you. He wants to meet you at church tomorrow, and if that goes well, he'll have you come to the shop Monday morning for an interview."

"Did you tell him about my past?" Rusty asked.

"No, I'll leave that to you, but I did tell him what a fine Christian man you are and that you have changed a lot since your youth. I don't think your past will keep him from hiring you. We'll pray for it."

Just as promised, when the service was over at church the next day, Mr. Howie brought his son over to meet Rusty. He was tall, broad shouldered, wearing kaki pants and a sweater. Clark seemed likeable, a chip off the old block. Their meeting lasted only a few minutes before he said, "Can you be at my place at 8:00 tomorrow morning?"

"Certainly. I'll be there."

Monday morning Mr. Howie came to Rusty's door and announced that since he didn't know where the cabinet shop was he would drive him for the interview. A good three miles from the Howies, they stopped at a large metal building with a sign that read "Clark's Woodworking: cabinets, trim, molding, miscellaneous." Inside they found Clark assigning work to the craftsmen. Then in a few minutes he invited Rusty into an office equipped with a computer, file cabinets, and a large desk covered with construction blue prints.

"Tell me what you can do in a cabinet shop, Rusty," Clark began.

"I want to be upfront with you," Sir, "and tell you about my past first," Rusty offered. He gave Clark the details about his past, omitting nothing. "Now if you haven't changed your mind about considering me for a job, I thank you. My only experience with woodworking was at Angola where we made lawn furniture, caskets, and other odds and ends."

"You made caskets?" Clark asked. "What did you do with them?"

"We used the cheaper ones for inmates who died there and had no other place to be buried, and some we sold. Dr. Billy Graham even bought one for his wife. It was really nice. I learned to use a planer, a table saw, routers, the drill press, gluing machine, nail guns, and sanders, just about everything in the shop. If I don't know how to use it, I'll learn."

"Do you drink or use drugs?"

"Not for more than six years now."

"If I hire you, will you be here every morning."

"Yes Sir, unless I am too sick."

"Do you get along well with others?"

"Since I was saved, my relationship with the Lord controls my relationship with others. Yes, I'll get along."

"Are you willing to take orders and follow directions?"

"Yes Sir."

"Why are you back in Winslow?" Clark asked.

"Well, Sir," he responded, "as I told you I was sent to prison for causing a serious injury to another young man, so I'm back here to find him and try to make amends."

"When can you begin work?"

"I'm ready now!" Rusty answered.

"Well, you are hired then. Come with me and I'll show you where to begin." Rusty thanked Clark's dad for the ride and he headed home alone.

Clark took him around and introduced him to the other workers, then assigned him to begin sanding some cabinet doors. It was probably everyone's least favorite job, but he was so proud to have a job that he was delighted to do it. In the days ahead he was assigned to various duties until he'd spent some time at every station in the shop.

Each morning he left home at least an hour early and walked to work; then he walked home in the afternoon, until one rainy afternoon when Joe saw him leave work walking and stopped to offer him a ride. When they arrived at the Howie's, he said, "Rusty, I had no idea you were walking this far to work every day. This is not far out of my way, so why don't you begin riding with me?"

"Thank you. I'd love that but I don't want to put you out," Rusty replied.

"Don't even think about it," he said. "Aren't we friends?"

"I sure think so," Rusty answered.

Joe provided his transportation faithfully until Clark began assigning Rusty the task of delivering finished cabinets, sometimes during the last hour of work. And he began going to job sites to take measurements before and after work. So he said, "Rusty, since you need the truck, you just keep that company truck at your place and you can drive it back and forth to work. And if you need it for some personal business, feel free to use it; you just buy the gas you use."

Rusty began asking everyone at work and those he called on if they knew the Applebys and if so where they lived. In fact, he found himself asking everyone he met. No one seemed to know them until finally one evening when he made a delivery and asked, the resident was willing to share all he knew. "Sure, I know them," he said. "I've known them for years. They used to live uptown, but after someone nearly killed Ben, he couldn't work and now his mother can only work part time, because it takes so much time caring for him, so they lost that house. Now they rent a small farm house out toward Harpersville. Someone has to be with him all time. He is fortunate to have his sisters."

"How many sisters are there?" Rusty asked.

"Well. Let's see. Lauren is the oldest. She is going to go to school to be a nurse, and she works part time at the TLC Nursing Home in the afternoon. She's about eighteen, I guess. Then Cathy is still in high school, but she plans to become a physical therapist. She has a part time job somewhere. While they are gone the mother, Marie, stays home to take care of Ben. Then when the girls get home, she goes to work as a barmaid at Smitty's. And for all of that they share one car."

"Can you tell me how to get to their house?" Rusty inquired.

"Sure. You take the next right on this road and follow it about four miles. You'll see a white frame house with blue shutters on the left of the road. The yard will probably be grown up and neglected because there are only two girls and the mother there, and they are always busy with Ben when they aren't working."

"Thank you," Rusty said. "I knew Ben before he was hurt and I'd like to see if I can help them someway."

"Good. They need all the help they can get," he added. "We try to help them some, but there is only so much we can do."

That very day, Rusty followed the directions and located the house. It was just as he had heard. The grass was tall and the house needed painting. An older model Nissan van was parked on the dirt driveway. Oh, how he wanted to stop, but he feared he would not be welcome. They must hate me, he thought, and for good reason. But the day was coming when he would need to get up the courage to stop and try to begin mending fences. He couldn't do it yet, though. He just didn't have the courage, so he drove on home, thinking about all the things they needed.

"Go and mend your fences," he remembered. And he'd been back in Winslow for some time but had done nothing about it. He had to do it. So on Saturday morning he drove into the Applepy's driveway and walked onto the porch and knocked on the door. After a minute Ben's middle-aged mother, who appeared to have just been aroused from sleep, opened the door.

"Good morning," Rusty said. "I hope I'm not disturbing you."

A flash of recognition crossed her face. "I know you. I remember you from that courtroom. You tried to kill my boy!" She was beginning to shout by then, and her daughters came running to the door. "Have you come to finish the job now?" she demanded.

"No Ma'm. I' just thought…".

"What are you doing out anyway?" Marie shouted. "Your seven years aren't up yet. Seven lousy years and you are not even having to serve all of them, but my son will suffer for the rest of his life because of you. Is that fair? You get away from here and don't let me ever see you again!"

Rusty knew that seeing him was too much of a shock and that he couldn't do anything then, and maybe never. But he began thinking of ways that he might help even without their permission. That tall grass, even though it was turning brown already, still needed cutting. So the next time he saw Wayne, the yardman, he hailed him and asked him to go cut it at his expense. "Now, Wayne," he cautioned, "Mrs. Appleby will not want you there, so when she sees you unloading your mower, she will object. You just tell her that a concerned neighbor wants to help them out. Then, when she demands to know who, you just tell here that you don't know my name, because you don't. After you finish, come by Clark's Woodworking and I'll pay you."

Wayne came the very next day and looked Rusty up at the shop. "How did it go?" Rusty asked.

He responded, "Those are proud folks. They didn't want me to cut the grass. Said they couldn't afford to pay. But I assured her that she wouldn't owe me anything; then I just started mowing. The grass was really high, so it took me longer than usual." Handing Rusty a bill, he said, "This is what you owe me, but I don't know why you are doing this."

"Just mending fences," Rusty responded.

Rusty felt such joy that he could actually begin to make amends for his transgressions. Although he never considered himself an alcoholic, he began to read about the twelve steps in the recovery process in order to be prepared to help others with addiction. Steps eight and nine spoke to his heart for they tell the recovering addict to make a list of all persons he had harmed and become willing to make amends to them all, and then begin to make amends wherever possible. Rusty realized that those steps applied to him also, for he had harmed some people, and a part of his recovery from guilt was to help them. So he continued to search for ways that he could help the Applebys.

Finally Rusty found the courage to call again at the Appleby home, but he was met with even greater hostility and threats: "If you come around here again, I'll shoot you," Mrs. Appleby shouted. "No, I don't want to kill you. That would be letting you off too easy. I want to cripple you for life just as you did my Ben. Now get away from here."

As Rusty backed out of the driveway, he noticed the propane tank in the back yard. The weather would soon be cold and the Applebys would need more propane to heat the house and cook with, so he visited the local propane dealer and asked if they knew where the Applebys live. "Yes, we know. In fact, she is one of our customers, but she has a hard time of it. Can't afford to fill her tank. Just buys the minimum every time."

"I would like to fill their tank with propane for them and keep it filled regularly" Rusty said. The dealer told him how much a full tank would cost, and he handed over the money. "Sir, there is one other thing," he said. "I don't want them to know who did it. If Mrs. Appleby objects to the delivery, just tell her that a neighbor just wants to help. It is not charity."

Every few days, Rusty began to buy two or three bags of groceries, and shortly before Marie was due to get home at midnight, he would park a quarter mile from the house and carry the groceries and carefully place them on the porch where she couldn't miss them. However, in a few days a deputy sheriff showed up at the shop as they were sitting down to lunch. He asked for Rusty Jenson and in front of everyone handed him an official notice that Mrs. Appleby has filed a restraining order against him. "You are not to go near her home," he said. "And if you do you will be arrested and sent back to prison."

Rusty didn't know that Clark had already told the crew the basic story of his incarceration and cautioned them to say nothing about it, so he decided that he needed to open up to them. He began, "fellows, there is something I need to tell you."

"Oh, we know that you got sent to prison and that you have paid you debt to society," Joe blurted out. "But we also see that you are a model citizen now, so you don't have to explain anything."

"But I want to tell you why I got this notice, Rusty continued. After I hurt Ben Appleby in a barroom brawl he has never recovered. In fact, he is paralyzed from the neck down. His family, a single mom and two sisters, have a rough time because at least one of them has to be with Ben at all times. Consequently, they are able to have only part time jobs, and the girls are still going to school. My reason for coming back to Winslow is to make amends for what I did and to help Ben and his family. I've been to their house twice and been threatened and run off both times. So this notice simply means that I can't go back until the restraining order expires. However, I am discovering ways that I can help them anonymously and am doing so."

"That's big of you, man," Bill said. "If they didn't want my help, I wouldn't give it."

"You don't understand. As a Christian I have a mandate from the Lord to love my neighbor and to minister to them. What I'm doing for them is also serving my Lord. And I believe that He will eventually open the door for us to bury the hatchet and be friends. Meanwhile, they need help and I intend to find a way to help them."

Clark spoke up, "Thank you, Rusty, for sharing that with us, and if we can help you to help them, you let us know. There is no restraining order against us. Now, let's get back to work." Everybody returned to his assigned task and no more was said about his situation.

When payday came Rusty took his check to the bank and spoke to a teller with whom he had become acquainted. "May I ask you something?" he asked.

"Certainly."

"Does Mrs. Appleby have an account here?"

"Well," she responded, "I'm not supposed to give out that information. Why do you want to know?"

"I know that she and her children don't have much income and they could use some help financially. I just want to deposit some money in her account anonymously."

"Oh! Since you will not be asking for her account number or personal information, I'll go out on a limb and tell you, yes, she does."

"Then I would like to deposit one-fourth of my paycheck in her account every week," Rusty said. "I do not want her to know where the money came from, but can you send her a receipt of the deposit?"

"Yes, we will do that. I must say that is very generous of you. Could I ask why you are doing it?"

"Just mending fences," he answered.

In what other ways could he help the Applebys, he wondered, then decided that he would drive past their house and look for something else he could do. As he traveled along the country road, he noticed Christmas decorations at every house until he came to the Applebys'. He could not even see a lighted Christmas tree by the window and an idea came to him. Maybe they couldn't afford one. Then he wondered if they would have anything to decorate one with. He immediately decided to buy them a tree and some lights. His next problem was how to get them to the Applebys.

Back in Winslow, he went to the discount store and bought Christmas tree lights and a few decorations. He asked for a box to put them in and the helpful clerk went to the store room and returned with one. Next he boxed them, taping the box securely, and addressed it to the Applebys. The next morning he mailed the package. Then he went to a Christmas tree lot and purchased a tree. That night, well after dark, when Mrs. Appleby had gone to work, he drove within a hundred yards of the house, parked, shouldered the tree, and walked quietly toward the house, where he gently placed it on the porch. Two nights later he drove past the house again and saw the lighted tree by the front window. It made him feel really good.

Still, I have to do more to seek Ben's, and his family's forgiveness and work to build a relationship with them, Rusty thought. This was helping but not getting their forgiveness.

Chapter 9

UNEXPECTED MIRACLES

Bewildered about the things that were being done for the family, Marie sat down with the girls to discuss it. "Lauren and Cathy, do you know who is doing all these things for us?"

"What things, Mom?"

"Well, let's see. Someone paid to have the yard mowed. The propane company has been filling our tank for free, claiming that a neighbor is paying for it. And deposits, which I haven't make, have been showing up in our bank account every month. We are finding groceries on the porch. Plus, the Christmas tree and decorations appeared mysteriously. As much as we need the help, I don't like to accept charity."

"I have no idea, Mom," Lauren responded.

"Me neither" Cathy added. "Maybe it's from Dad. I wish he would take more interest in our welfare."

"No it isn't," Marie responded. "He won't do anything for us. Besides, I called and asked him and he said 'definitely not.' And I just can't believe any of our neighbors are doing it. We hardly know them, and they have never done anything for us before. None of our old neighbors in the garden district seem to even care about us now that we have no money. If you aren't in their inner circle, they have nothing to do with you, and we certainly aren't in their circle of friends. They haven't even called to check on us. I asked Smitty, but he denies doing it, and I believe him. He has never done anything special for me except to help us move. And none of the patrons at the bar like me well enough to do anything for me. Besides, they're wasting all of their money in the bar every night. I can't imagine people being so irresponsible that they are neglecting their families the way they do. I just don't know what to make of it. Of course, it really is a big help. I don't know what we would do without it."

"Do you think it could be Rusty who is doing it?" Lauren inquired.

"God, I hope not. If it came from him, I want to send it back. I don't want his help or to ever see him again. Besides, I doubt that he is making enough at that cabinet shop to do so much for us. Let's ask among our friends and see if anyone knows. You know there are no secrets in Winslow. Rumors spread like wildfire, so if one person knows something, it's soon all over town. You remember how quickly the news spread about your father walking out on us. The jerk! Then when we lost the house everyone knew it almost before we did. If you hear anything, let me know." They had never stopped to consider that the things they had prayed for might be happening. Of course, not everything they sought had occurred, but answers were coming in unexpected ways.

Shouts came from the bedroom. It was Ben, of course, wanting to get out of bed and into his chair. When Marie and his sisters entered his room, he demanded, "What have you all been whispering about? Are you talking about me again?"

"No, Ben," Marie said, "you are not the only topic of conversation around here."

"But you are always complaining about me. I hear you."

"No, we are not complaining. We might discuss how best to care for you, but we are not complaining. We're doing everything we can to meet your needs. I just wish we could do more. You know that if we didn't love you and want to care for you, we could stick you in a nursing home and forget you, like so many others are doing with their loved ones."

Even though Ben had a television in his room, he had come to enjoy sitting in his chair in the living room and watching TV with the girls. The noise interfered with the girls' concentration on their homework, but they didn't dare complain to Ben or suggest that he turn it off. In addition, they were still afraid to try to transfer him to the bed alone. So they had to stay awake until Marie got home after midnight for her to help get him into bed, and that made them sleepy students the next morning. Ben could sleep until noon, so it was not a problem for him.

Life went on for the Applebys. It was not easy but they were adjusting to having less, working harder, and sacrificing personal time for Ben's sake. Sadly they couldn't anticipate a time when things would be better.

Chapter 10

An Open Door

Rusty had become very involved in the First Church. Despite his story, which had circulated through the congregation, no doubt, he was accepted because of his obvious conversion and rehabilitation. In fact, he was called upon to pray in the services, to substitute for an absentee teacher in Sunday school, and to be a greeter at the front door. Then one day the pastor asked him to come by his office after the service. When he arrived, Pastor Williams informed him of a ministry the church sponsored at the TLC Nursing Home which needed some help. Every Thursday at the time of the evening meal a small group from the church led a short worship service in the dining hall. The person who had been delivering a brief devotion was moving out of town, and he asked if Rusty could be the new speaker. He was assured that someone else would sing, and all he would need to do was the devotional. With some reservation, Rusty accepted the responsibility and promised to be there at 5:30 on Thursdays.

At first he failed to see that God was opening a door for him to associate with one of the Applebys. Then he remembered hearing that Lauren worked there in the afternoon after school. Maybe she would still be there at 5:30. And maybe he would get to see her, but he hoped that she didn't recognize him for a while.

Rusty spent hours preparing his first devotional for the residents of the nursing home. He thought it best to begin that ministry with a brief testimony of his Christian life, leaving out, however, his crime and the Angola experience. When he arrived at the home, attendants were bringing patients into the dining hall. Even though he didn't know Lauren yet, since he had seen her only once, he thought that she must be the pretty young woman pushing wheel chairs and carrying on friendly conversations with the patients. When the service began the attendants stayed to help as needed. They wore name tags but he still had not seen one with Lauren on it.

After three songs with the residents and a solo, Rusty went to the podium for the ten-minute message. "I want to begin with my testimony," he began. "You need to know who I am before you hear what I have to say. Then he shared what the Lord had done for him and how his relationship with Him and fellowship with Him were the most important things in his life. He followed with a call to be thankful, "Instead of mourning the loss of something, be thankful for what we have," he said. Some of the residents dozed and some seemed too bewildered to understand, but a few nodded in agreement and thanked him at the end. "I'll be back next week," he promised.

Week after week he continued to speak at the home, where he soon identified the attractive young lady as Lauren by her name tag, but she avoided him like the plague. She must have recognized him, he thought. Three months passed before Lauren came by at the close of the service and complimented him and the devotional and thanked him for coming every week. Although they still were not introduced, they both seemed to be sure who the other was.

One afternoon Rusty bravely introduced himself to Lauren. She said, "I think I know who you are. Aren't you the Rusty who injured my brother?"

"Yes." He confessed and said, "I am so sorry. In fact, the reason I came back to Winslow is to try to make up for what I did. I so want to apologize to Ben and ask his forgiveness, but your mother doesn't allow me to come to the house, and I understand that. I know you are all suffering because of me."

"I know that you have come there twice, but my mother has so much hatred toward you; I guess we all do. But to tell you the truth, I think we need to leave it all behind us and seek to be healed. Hatred is not going to change Ben's condition. But I have to tell you, he is far from forgiving you. I honestly don't know if he ever will."

"Well, I want you to know that I'm praying for him."

"Pray all you want, but I doubt if it will do any good," she replied. "He is so bitter. I guess we all are. Our father has left us because of Ben's condition. We lost our house in the garden district. My mother has to work nights in a bar. We all are having to sacrifice."

After that, every week Lauren and Rusty would speak and talk briefly. Finally, she told him, "I'm trying to get Mother to allow you to come to visit Ben, but she is not able yet. If you ever get to come it will have to be while she is at work. She doesn't ever want to see you. Even if you come I think Ben will just curse you and demand that you leave. However, he can't do anything else to hurt you."

Months later, Rusty stayed and visited at the nursing home for a while after the service; then when he went out the door, there stood Lauren, as if she were waiting for a ride. "Is everything all right?" he asked.

"I don't know," she said. "I'm afraid something is wrong. We all share one car, and my sister was supposed to come get me when I got off work, but she hasn't arrived. I hope nothing is wrong."

"I hope that too," he responded. "Would you like me to drive you home?"

"I don't think that would be a good idea. I think I'll wait a little longer."

"Then let me wait with you," he suggested.

A half hour later, it was obvious that something was wrong, and Lauren agreed to allow him to drive her home. But first she told the nursing home staff if her sister came for her to tell her that she found another ride home. "It's so late my mother will probably have caught a ride with a coworker by now, leaving Ben home alone. I do hope that my sister has called her."

As they drove to her home, Lauren said, "I really appreciate the messages you have been bringing, especially when you talk about you faith. I need that."

"When you are ready," he responded, "we can talk more about it."

"Someday, maybe," she said.

As they topped a hill, they noticed a van in the ditch. Lauren shouted, "Stop! That's our car. Someone's still in it; it must be Cathy." Lauren jumped out of the truck almost before it stopped, calling, "Cathy, Cathy."

The window lowered and Cathy answered., "Hey, I'm here."

"Are you hurt? Why are you still sitting here in the car after dark?"

"I was afraid to get out, just hoping that some friend would stop to help me."

By this time Rusty stood beside Lauren and she introduced them to each other. "What are doing with him, Lauren?" Cathy asked.

Lauren explained that Rusty had rescued her and that they would now take Cathy home too. "Can you give us both a ride, Rusty?"

"Yes, I'll be happy too. But do you want me to try to pull your van out first?"

"Do you think you can?"

"I believe so; then we will have to see if it's damaged in any way."

"I don't believe it is," Cathy spoke. "I was just forced off the road by an oncoming car and slid into the ditch."

Rusty took a tow strap from the tool box and fastened it between the van and the truck and carefully pulled it from the ditch. After examining it, he said, "I believe you are right. I don't see any damage."

Cathy slid into the driver's seat, and Lauren said, "Rusty, I'll ride on home with her."

"Then I'll follow you to be sure you get home all right."

"Okay, but, Rusty, please don't stop and come in. I'm afraid you would not be welcome."

Rusty continued to talk with Lauren every week at the nursing home. In addition to being lovely, he discovered that she was very intelligent. She told him that she chose to be a nurse because of Ben's injuries and treatment, and that she hoped to be able to work in a rehab center. In a couple of years she will have completed school and be ready for an internship. As they talked one day, Lauren asked, "Rusty, are you the one who has been doing all those things for us?'

"What kind of things?" he responded.

"Someone has been putting money in our checking account regularly and buying propane for us plus leaving a Christmas tree and bags of groceries on the porch. When we try to find out who is doing it, the only answer we get is 'a neighbor.' I assure you that no 'neighbor' has done anything for us until you came to town. So I've figured out that it has to be you. Is it?"

"Well, I can't lie. I have done those things, but don't tell anybody, please."

"We really appreciate it. But I can tell you now that if my mother knew it was you, she wouldn't like it. She doesn't like charity and she would like it even less if she knew it came from you."

He responded, "I don't consider it charity."

"Then what do you call it? And why are you doing it?" she demanded.

"First, I consider myself paying a debt. Second, I'm trying to make amends. I would like to build a relationship with your family, and someday I hope to help Ben forgive me. Finally, I believe that it is what God wants me to do."

"Do you believe that God communicated His will to you, then?"

"Yes, I do. It all began before I left Angola. My Christian warden told me to 'Go and mend my fences.' Somehow I've felt that was more than an admonition from the warden, so I believe that God has sent me on this mission."

"I don't know," Lauren said. "I'm not sure God cares about us. We prayed and asked for Ben to be healed, and we've prayed for help for our situation. I just have trouble believing in a God who cares and acts."

"Have you considered that I might be part of the answer to your prayers?" Rusty asked.

"Well, no, I haven't."

"Lauren, do you think that it's possible for me to visit Ben sometime?"

"I doubt it."

"But you can help me to if you will."

"You don't understand, Rusty. You just don't know how much Ben and my mother resent you. They would never welcome you. However, I have been trying to broach the subject since you first came to the house, but I don't think I'm making any progress. You just don't understand what you've cost us. We have to rent a substandard house; we all have to work to make ends meet; and one of us has to be with Ben all the time. You can't imagine how difficult it is to have to take care of the personal needs of your own brother."

"Lauren, I can't really say that, 'I know,' but with all that is in me I am really sorry. If I could do anything to undo what happened to Ben I would gladly do it. But since I can't undo it, I wish I could make life easier for you all. Help me to help you. Tell me what I can do. And help me to build a relationship."

"I'll do what I can, but don't count on much change," she responded.

A little bit later Rusty decided to drive by the Appleby house one Saturday. As he approached the house, he saw that something was wrong. Mother and daughters were in the yard at the edge of the porch, and the motorized chair and Ben lay on the ground. All three ladies were flagging him down. They probably couldn't tell who they were calling on for help, but they were so desperate for help that they were frantically waving at any passerby.

Rusty drove into the driveway and jumped out of the truck. When Mrs. Appleby saw him, her face fell, and she said, "Oh, it's you!" He knew then that she would not allow him to help if it weren't such a difficult situation. They explained that Ben wanted to come out on the porch and they opened the door for him, and he accidentally ran off of the porch. They were having trouble lifting the heavy chair, to say nothing of Ben's dead weight of over two hundred pounds.

With their help Rusty struggled to lift the chair onto the porch. Then the question was how to get Ben into the chair. He knew that it would probably be impossible for him to lift that much weight, but he had to try, so he prayed for extra strength, and while Lauren and Cathy held the chair at the edge of the porch, he picked Ben up and sat him in the chair. "Thank You, Lord," he prayed silently.

After getting Ben into the house, Lauren examined him to be sure that he wasn't injured and said, "I think he is okay. Are you all right, Ben?" she asked.

With anger in his voice, Ben responded, "Yeah. You know I don't feel anything below my neck. You should have just left me there to die. Because of this do-gooder I have nothing left to live for."

"Hello, Ben," Rusty said. "I'm glad you are okay. Someday when you feel like it I'd like to visit with you. Do you think that would be okay?"

"Never!" he shouted. "Now go."

Mrs. Appleby followed him to the porch and said, "We thank you for helping us this time, but we don't want you here again. We will manage on our own."

"Okay," he said, "but just know that if I can ever help you, all you have to do is let me know."

"It would have to an emergency," Marie said.

Back in the truck, Rusty said, "Thank You Lord for providing me a crack in the door. I know it's a small opening, but it is a beginning. I pray that you will give me more opportunities." As he drove back to town, he wondered how those ladies could transfer Ben from his chair to the bed and back to the chair, so he decided to ask Lauren the next Thursday.

"It's really hard," Lauren said. "It takes at least two of us. We have to stand him erect, then twist him around and ease him onto the bed where we can slide him around to a good position. He grumbles the whole time and curses you for putting him in this condition. I'm sorry."

"I notice that they have some lifts for that purpose here at the home. Do you think that would be a help to you?"

"I'm sure it would," she responded, "but they are very expensive, and we can never afford one."

"I see," he answered. "Well, let just ask God for one."

"You go ahead. My prayers don't seem to reach the ceiling."

Rusty prayed for a lift during the weekend and checked on the cost, which was way beyond his means. However, unwilling to give up, he continued to pray for a solution to the problem and the Lord seemed to be saying, "ask others."

The logical place to begin was with his employer who, after all, had once offered to help. So he went into Clark's office and broached the subject. "How much would it cost?" he asked. But when Rusty told him, he merely said, "Wow, that much huh? Let me think about it." Rusty knew that often meant "no," but he was determined that he wouldn't give up yet.

Next he called on the pastor at First Church and asked him if the church could help. "How much will it cost?" Pastor Williams asked. It seemed to Rusty that everything boiled down to cost instead of need. However, he reminded himself that this wasn't their problem. It was his fence to mend. However, the pastor said, "We do have a small benevolence fund I might tap for a little money. Maybe I can get some others to help also," he volunteered.

Finally Rusty went to the hospital and asked the administrator if there was some agency which helps with that sort of thing. He told him, "The Red Cross and the local Aid Society might give you some help, but I doubt it." However, when Rusty contacted them, both offered limited help.

He prayed all week for the help he would need. Then the next Sunday, the pastor asked Rusty to stay after the service. "I contacted a couple of wealthy men in our church," he began, "and they've both agreed to help. That, along with our church contribution will provide about half the funds." Then the Aid Society came through with a sizeable donation.

Finally, the very next Monday morning, Clark called Rusty into his office and said, "Rusty, I've been bothered all weekend about your request. Have you received any other help?"

"Yes," he replied, "I now have a promise of about 60% of the cost, and I think I can handle 15% of it."

"So that leaves 25%," Clark responded. "I'll tell you, Rusty, because you're doing such a good thing, I'm going to provide the rest of it. And whatever you need to set up for its use – assembly, adjustments to the house, or whatever – I'll take our crew and get it done. How does that sound?"

"It sounds like God has come through with a miracle. Just wait until I tell Lauren," Rusty responded gleefully.

Even though it wasn't Thursday, after work Rusty went by to see Lauren, and when she had a chance to talk, he told her, "I have good news."

"What's that?" she asked. "Did you win the lottery or something?"

"Better than that; I got an answer to prayer. We're getting you a lift. I'll order it tomorrow if you agree."

"How in the world could you afford that?"

"Well, I have some help, but behind it all is God, who moved on the hearts of some others who obeyed and contributed. Isn't that wonderful?"

With tears in her eyes, she said, "Yes, it is. But, Rusty, before you order it I'd better tell my mother about this. She will have to agree to it."

"Of course, she will have to know. But you don't have to name names; just tell her that some caring people want to do it."

The next morning Rusty was at the university when Lauren arrived, waiting for her mother's response. "Tell me that your mother agreed, please."

"Well, she was reluctant and asked if you are behind this, trying to salve your conscience. I had to tell her that you are but that you have enlisted help from others too. Finally, she said, 'yes.' just because it will help you girls get Ben in bed at night when I'm working I'll agree to it."

At work the next morning, Clark allowed Rusty to use the telephone to make some calls to those who were contributing. Then he ran into a snag when he called to order it. They demanded payment up front or a company to bill it to. Even though that worried Rusty, when Clark heard about it, he had no problem with it. "Just order it in the company name," he volunteered. He was assured that it would be delivered within ten days. And Clark promised that the first Saturday after its arrival, he would ask some of his crew to help install it.

They worked diligently at the shop for the next ten days, but Rusty would still head to the nursing home every day after work to see Lauren. He would offer to drive Lauren home but she always said no because it might cause an uproar at home. The lift arrived as promised on Thursday and Rusty presented the invoice to all of the donors, and every one of them came through with their contribution. Even old Mr. Howie, when he learned what Rusty was up to, insisted that he be allowed to pay Rusty's 15%. "The lift is here and paid for," Rusty announced to Lauren that evening, and Clark is planning to bring part of his crew to assembly it and make whatever adjustments have to be made to the room on Saturday."

"That's great," Lauren said, "but you had better let me talk to Ben and my mother; they might not allow you in the house."

"Okay, but I plan to be there, as close as I can get to the action."

Friday evening Lauren said Rusty could come with the crew for the installation. "Praise God!" he shouted. At least he would be getting into the house.

Saturday morning four of them showed up at the Appleby house and began to assess the situation. Because of its size, they had to assembly the lift in the bedroom itself, but then they discovered that Ben's room was too small. They were baffled about what to do. They couldn't enlarge the room. However, when Lauren saw their dilemma she offered a suggestion. "Our room is a little larger. Let's look to see if it will work. Cathy and I will be willing to switch rooms with Ben." After measuring the room Rusty discovered that was a viable solution. Although he regretted the sacrifice the girls would have to make, he appreciated Lauren even more for her willingness to do so. By noon the rooms had been switched and an experiment with the equipment performed. It promised to be a big help.

The Applebys thanked the other men for their help, ignoring Rusty's part. But as the others left, he hung back, and Ben asked, "Rusty, why are you doing this? You must know that I hate you."

"Well," Ben, "Lauren asked me the same question, so I'll tell you as I told her. I'm extremely sorry for what happened to you. If I could change it or even trade places with you I would. But since I can't I am trying to make things a little better for you and your family. I can't make you well, but I'd like to build a helpful relationship with you. And I would like your forgiveness."

"That's not possible," he responded. "I can never forgive you. You don't deserve it."

"You know, Ben, I got off light, but remember that I paid a price, too. Being in Angola for five long years wasn't a piece of cake. I suffered too."

"But," he said, "there is no comparison. Can you even imagine what it is like to know that you will never walk again or hold a job? You don't know how it is to be dependent on others for everything, hating everything that you have to receive from them. You can't possibly know what it's like for a twenty-three-year-old to have to wear a diaper and allow his sisters and mother to change it. Listen, Bud, I do want to hear how you suffered living off the taxpayers with a roof over your head and food on the table. I hope the experience was demeaning to you. I want to hear how you were beaten up and raped at Angola. I want to rejoice over every bit of suffering you endured."

"Anytime you're ready," Rusty agreed.

"Well, I'll think about it and someday I'll let you tell me. But I can't stand the sight of you yet. So get out of our house."

As Rusty left, Mrs. Appleby followed him onto the porch and said, "Young man, don't think this is the beginning of a good relationship. I understand also that you are spending time talking to Lauren. I warn you that you are not going to hurt her and get away with it. I'll kill you if you do. Do you understand me?"

"Yes, Mrs. Appleby," he answered her. "Let me assure you that I do not intend to hurt Lauren or any of your family."

Rusty dreamed of the day when things would be better in his life. He wanted to succeed at something, have a good job, own a home, get married and have a family. But for the present his life was consumed with mending fences. He caught himself and scolded and said aloud to himself, "Don't you remember what you told those people at the nursing home? Be grateful for what you have! You have your freedom, a job, a place to live, and friends. Be grateful." It was true that he had the best relationship possible with his employer and co-workers. He treasured his relationship with the Lord most of all. First Church had come to be a haven for him and a place to serve. Still he had an insatiable desire to become all he could be and to do as much Christian service as possible. Still, he was praying for greater success in every area.

Then one sunny, spring day, he was helping his landlord prepare a flower garden for planting. Mrs. Howie was supervising and planning where to plant everything. "Hello," someone called, "anybody home?" He recognized the voice as Clark's, who was already coming around the house to the back yard.

"Well, good morning," Mrs. Howie greeted him with a hug. Then he and his father shared a hearty handshake. Immediately Mrs. Howie volunteered, "Let me go make us some coffee. These men have earned one." She hastened in to the house and before long she emerged with a tray filled with coffee and some old fashioned teacakes. "Come, let's sit on the porch," she called. They sat and visited while enjoying the refreshments and catching up on the news.

Finally, Clark turned to Rusty and asked, "Can I speak with you in private, Rusty?"

"Certainly," he answered, worrying that he'd done something wrong at work. "Let's go to the house."

Inside, Clark looked around and said, "You are keeping this place mighty clean. Say, I'm glad that you are here, and I appreciate the way you help out my parents."

"Thank you, Clark. I'm the one who should be grateful, however."

"Rusty," he began, "I need to talk with you about something very important and I'd like you to give it some thought. I'm nearing retirement age and I want to slow down at work, so I want to name you foreman. I want you to learn as much as possible about every part of the business so you can supervise everything."

Shocked, Rusty replied, "Gosh I don't know what to say, Clark, but I thank you for this kind of confidence in me. What about the other men? Shouldn't one of them have that job? They've worked for you much longer than I have. I would hate for them to resent me as foreman."

"Yes, that's all true, but I've watched all of you while anticipating this day, and, Rusty, I'm convinced that you are the best man for the job. You've learned fast. You work hard. You get along well with the customers and your co-workers. Regardless of your past, you have a good heart. And you are willing to do anything that is needed. I like that, so you let me worry about the other men. I'll explain everything to them. Will you take the job?"

"Yes," he answered. "Even though it will be a big responsibility; however, it's such a great opportunity that I don't even have to think about it or pray about it. Thank you."

"Well, Rusty, I thought you would be pleased, but that isn't what you need to be thinking and praying about."

"You mean there is more."

"Yes. When I retire, I would like to sell you the business. You will have had four or five years to prepare yourself as you promote the business and manage much of it, so by then you will be able to own it and run it."

"Gosh," he responded, "I can't believe God works so fast. Would you believe that I've just been praying about my future? But you know, Clark, that I don't have anything to pay for it with, and I could never borrow enough to buy it. I wish I could but I don't see how. However, I'm willing to pray for God to make it possible."

"You sure have lots of faith, Rusty. I know that you haven't had time to pray about it yet or to turn it over to God and watch Him work. So you prepare yourself and pray earnestly about it and we will see what happens. Okay?"

"Sure. Thank you." Clark left him astounded at the turn of events. He couldn't believe it. But in his mind he was thinking, "Thank You, Lord. That's one prayer answered."

As if that weren't enough of a shock, another was on its way. When the mail came, Mrs. Howie came bringing him a piece of mail, the first he had received since coming back to Winslow. Mrs. Howie teased him about the pink envelope, "Oh, Rusty, it's pink and smells like jasmine. It has to be from a girl. Have you been holding something from us?"

"No, I promise." he defended himself. "I don't know who it could be from." There was no return address, and he couldn't open it until a while after Mrs. Howie left. Then when he could stand the suspense no longer, he tore the envelope open, and looked first at the signature and discovered to his surprise that it was from Lauren. It was just a note, but if it had no more than her name he would have been thrilled. But there was more:

Thank you, Rusty, for securing the lift and installing it. You have been very kind to us and more than generous. I'm sorry that you aren't allowed to visit at our house, but I do so enjoy the little time that we get to spend together. Thanks again.

> *Sincerely,*
> *Lauren, your friend*
> *p.s. I hope to see you Thursday.*

It had been a while coming, but things were looking up for Rusty. He loved Clark and appreciated his offer more than he knew, but it was with fear and trepidation that he faced the future. He decided the best he could do was leave it in God's hands and accept whatever He worked out. Rusty's budding relationship with Lauren was even more surprising and rewarding. He knew that it hadn't grown much yet, but he was beginning to develop special feelings for her, and he believed she was accepting him. Aloud, he admitted, "It's just unbelievable, given my past, that Lauren would even accept me as a friend, but that is the way she signed the note. Thank You! Thank You, Lord! Only You could have done this. It's a miracle, another prayer answered." He couldn't wait until Thursday, so he went to the nursing home Monday.

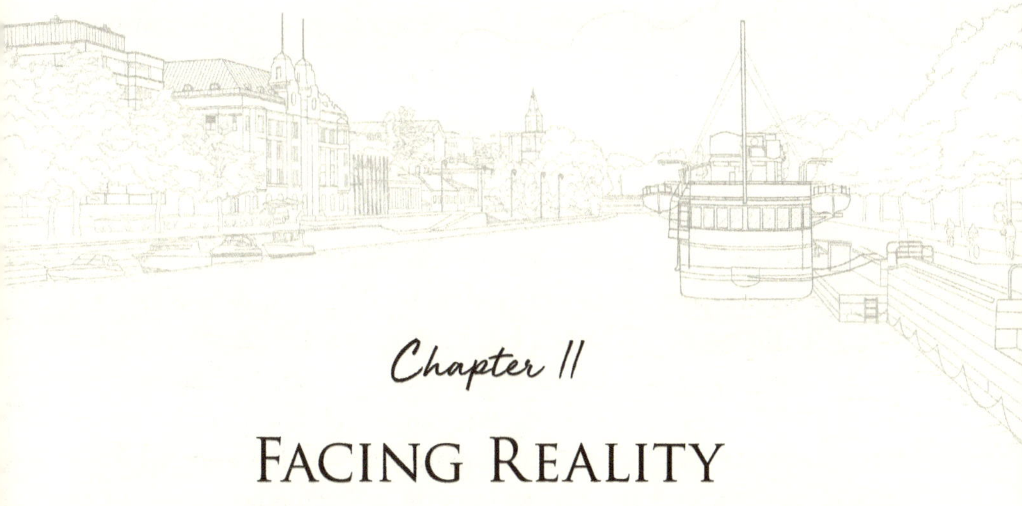

Chapter 11

FACING REALITY

While enjoying a Saturday morning breakfast of bacon and eggs, toast and jelly with orange juice and milk, Lauren broke the silence and created a firestorm. "Mom, I need to tell you something. Rusty has been very helpful to us and we have become good friends. I know you don't approve but I truly believe that he has changed and that he wants to be closer to all of us."

"No. I won't have it," Marie huffed. "I don't want you to be friends with him either, and he is not going to be closer to me. I don't want you to even talk to him."

"Mom, there is something else: he has invited me to drive up to the lake with him for a picnic this afternoon, and I want to go," Lauren pleaded.

"No, you can't go."

"Listen, Mom. I'm twenty-one years old and I've never had a serious date. I'm about to graduate from college. Cathy and I have sacrificed our teen years because of our family tragedy and we've been glad to do it. We've tried never to show it, but we feel deprived of a normal life. We want to help you with Ben, but we want some liberty as well. I'm sorry if I'll have to disobey you, but I am an adult and I am going on the picnic with Rusty."

"You may, but it will be over my strongest objection. And I don't know if you will be able to come back here if you do."

69

"Mom, you can't mean that! You and Cathy mean the most to me, and you need me here. However, I can manage to get a place to stay until I graduate if I have to; then, with a good job, I can get my own place, but I'm not willing to burden you and Cathy any more. Cathy has not been able to go to the school prom, nor date either. She is suffering too. And while we are at it, I may as well say what's on my mind."

"It looks like you've done it already," Marie complained.

"No, Mom, there's more. In my nursing psychology class my professor said that to hate and refuse to forgive hurts the person who is doing it more than the person she hates. I know you want to hurt Rusty, but really you are just hurting yourself. At the same time you are feeding the same attitude in Ben. We need to model forgiveness and show him that he can make the best of his situation. This is destroying you. I'm sorry to have to tell you this, but you have changed from the loving mother you were into a slave to your emotions."

"You friend Rusty has done this to me," Marie argued.

"No, Mom, Rusty hurt Ben and all of us, but it's not what he did that is destroying us. It's our response to what he did. I know you love Ben and want to care for him always, but what will happen to him if you ruin your own life and his? You are just encouraging his hatred. Shouldn't we be trying to help him get over this and make the best of what life he has?"

"I'm sorry, but I just can't do it. Not yet anyway."

With tears streaming down her cheeks, Cathy pleaded, "Please, Mom. We need our old mom back. This anger and hatred has destroyed the loving mother you were." By then all three of the ladies were crying, and Marie stood to hug them and promise to change. "I don't know how I've hurt you, but I'll try to do better."

"Rusty will be here at 2:00. Could we possibly allow him to come knock on the door and step inside for me? Maybe he can even speak to Ben. I've told him that we have to be back before time for you to go to work, Mom. Okay?"

"I guess it will have to be. It looks like you are becoming the mom, telling me what to do," Marie grumbled and stormed out of the room. Lauren and Cathy just looked at each other and shook their heads.

Lauren knocked on Ben's door and entered to tell him that Rusty was coming to take her on a picnic. "No, you can't do it," he insisted.

"Ben, I'm not asking your permission. I'm simply telling you. If he comes in could you at least speak to him and be civil?"

"Was he civil to me when he swung that chair?"

"No. But Ben we have to leave all of that behind us. Rusty wants to be more than civil now, and he has been very helpful to us. You just think about it and try to be friendly to him." Without another word from Ben, Lauren walked out of the room.

When Rusty arrived and knocked on the door, Lauren went to open it. "Hello, Rusty. Come in." Both Marie and Ben were closed up in their rooms.

Rusty asked, "May I go in and speak to Ben?"

"Yes," Lauren responded. "But he may not speak to you. In fact, he might not let you in his room."

"That's all right. I'll just knock on his door and see."

"Who is it?" Ben asked.

"Rusty."

"What do you want? Have you come to gloat over my condition?" After a long pause, Ben said, "The door's open."

Rusty stepped into the room with a greeting, "Hello, Ben. Thank you for letting me in. I'm glad to see you."

"Well, you've seen me, so close the door on your way out."

"Goodbye then Ben. I'll see you again soon," Rusty said as he exited the room and closed the door softly.

Lauren and Rusty enjoyed a pleasant afternoon, and Lauren told him what had transpired between her and Marie at the house earlier. "I'm not sure it's progress yet; however, it's a first step."

"Great," Rusty responded. "I was surprised that I was able to get into Ben's room to speak to him. That's progress. Thank you so much for taking the initiative in this matter. I think you are exactly right about who is hurting whom. Of course, I feel terrible that your mother and Ben are angry and unforgiving, but I'm just sorry for what they are doing to themselves and that it all reverts back to me."

"Well," Lauren changed the subject, "let's not talk about it anymore. Let's enjoy this beautiful setting and the lovely weather. You know I haven't been here in at least six years."

About 4:00 Ben went to the truck and brought back a picnic basket filled with drinks and food. He had neat containers filled with fried chicken, rolls, a salad, and two pieces of cake. "Don't tell me you cooked all of this yourself," Lauren teased.

"Why? Don't you think I can cook? I worked in the kitchen for a year at the 'plantation.' Surely I learned something" he joked. "However, to be truthful, I washed dishes and pots and pans the entire time. I made the mistake of telling Mrs. Howie about our picnic, so she insisted on preparing the food for us. So it won't poison you."

When the meal was finished they took a stroll along the sandy shoreline watching the ducks swim and dip under the water. Timidly, Rusty reached for Lauren's hand and to his delight she responded by gripping his. It was a wonderful afternoon and Lauren told him that she enjoyed it, so Rusty asked, "Do you think we could spend more time together?"

"I would love that," Lauren responded, "but you know that I go to school, then work, and afterward have to be home with Ben. I don't know when we could be together."

"Do you think I might be able to visit you at home some evenings, and since you mother and Cathy are home on Sundays, maybe we can do something then. Say, I go to church every Sunday, so why don't you come with me?"

"I don't know. I'm not much of a church person," Lauren said. But I am pleased that you go, and I appreciate your strong faith and commitment. If things get better at home I may be able to do something with you on Sunday afternoon, if you wish."

Back at the Appleby home, Rusty walked Lauren to the door, but she didn't invite him in, and no one else was in sight. Driving away, Rusty's heart was overflowing, and he was singing "I've got peace like a river in my soul" all the way to town.

That evening when they sat down to dinner, Marie told the girls how sorry she was that she had denied them so much. She promised to do better and to work at accepting and forgiving Rusty. "After all, it looks like he is going to be underfoot around here. And I'll try to show Ben how to forgive and leave it behind us. I guess I should thank you girls for setting me straight."

"Never mind, Mom," Lauren said. "We know you have been doing the best you can."

"Well, from now on, if one of you is here with Ben, the other can do some things you would like to do."

Chapter 12

RELIVING THE PAST

At Clark's Woodworking, things were going well. With Clark's experienced guidance, Rusty's enthusiasm, and the exceptional quality of their finished products, the business was growing by leaps and bounds. Every one of the employees had accepted Rusty as foreman and they worked well together. Clark had started Rusty on a profit-sharing plan, so since he had little personal expenses other than helping the Applebys, he was building quite a little nest egg. Already he was thinking of a time when he could be married and build a house of his own. And he was sure that he had found the woman to share the rest of his life if he could just convince her.

Unfortunately, Clark's wife had been diagnosed with Parkinson's disease which meant that Clark had to be away from the business more and more, so he reminded Rusty occasionally of his plans to retire and sell the business to him; therefore, Rusty was learning as much as possible about the management of the business as well as the mechanics of it. He had an experienced and dependable crew who had worked for Clark for a long time and he hoped that he could keep every one of them.

Rusty's fellow workmen had learned of his growing involvement with Lauren and teased him mercilessly. Every morning when he came to work they would ply him with questions about what he did the night before. He would just smile and go about his work. But they could tell that he was enjoying every minute of it. "It won't be long before you will be sporting a ring on that left hand, and then you have someone to answer to. She'll soon have you asking 'how high' when she tells you to jump. Then the first thing you know there be some little ones crying 'Daddy'. " His only hope was that he could just make it happen, for he still couldn't believe that Lauren would accept him.

One day Mrs. Appleby's landlord came in to Clark's and said that she had been complaining to him about the limited cabinet space in the house and demanding that he add more. He was finally giving in and wanted Clark to go to the house and see what she needed and build and install them. Since Clark was preoccupied, he suggested that Rusty go. Rusty was delighted because this would give him a legitimate reason to go. However, he waited until Lauren was home so he could see her as well.

Marie could hardly deny him admission, so Rusty used Lauren to inform the others and set up a convenient time for his initial visit to take measurements and find out what they wanted. "I'm sure," Lauren said, "that Saturday is not a work day for you, but do you think you could come on Saturday?"

"Sure. Is this Saturday all right?"

"I think so, but I'll check to make sure," she replied. She soon called Rusty and gave him the okay, so they planned the visit for 11:00 on the next Saturday. "Rusty, if you can stay for lunch, I'll try to cook us something, and that will extend your visit some."

"That sounds great." Rusty replied. "I'll be there."

Saturday morning Rusty dressed in his best work clothes and drove out to the Applebys. Cathy met him at the door, saying, "Lauren is busy cooking, so come in. I'll get Mom to show you what she wants."

Marie seemed cool toward Rusty but more accepting of him than ever before. Rusty let her describe what she wanted, and then he took the necessary measurements. Then while waiting for the meal to be finished, he walked through the open door to Ben's room and found him watching television. "Hello, Ben, how are you today?"

"Besides being crippled, paralyzed, helpless, and angry, I'm making it." Again, that was Ben's best reception.

"I'm here to measure for some new kitchen cabinets, and Lauren has invited me to stay for lunch."

"You had better watch it, she may poison you," Ben smiled. "Or if she don't I may. She's not much of a cook you know."

"You wouldn't do that to me would you, Ben?"

"If I could I might. But I can't reach the poison," Ben said with a grin.

Lauren came to the door to say, "It's ready. Ben I heard what you said. Shame on you."

As Rusty and Lauren left the room, Ben didn't move, so Rusty asked, "Aren't you coming, Ben?

"We usually feed him later in here," Lauren answered.

"Ben, why don't you come to the table with us today? I'll even feed you."

"Huh, in that case you might poison me." But to Lauren's surprise, Ben began to maneuver his chair toward the table.

Marie had come into the room also. Surprised to see Ben, she said, "Why don't you sit at the end, Ben, like the head of the house."

"Yea! I'll be the head, a helpless head."

Rusty knew that Ben must be embarrassed that someone had to feed him, so he helped to relieve a little of the shame. When the meal was finished, Rusty bragged on Lauren's cooking and thanked her for lunch. She beamed. But Ben wouldn't let it go. "It'll do," he said.

"Well, you ate plenty of it I noticed. So you should be saying 'thank you.'"

"I guess. Thank you chef Lauren. Now give me some water…please."

Rusty promised to have the cabinets finished in a week and he and a couple of workers would come and install them. Maybe he could get someone to help him one evening or on the next Saturday. As he started to leave, Lauren followed him to the truck and thanked him. Then, instead of going home, Rusty went straight to the shop and began laying out the pattern for the cabinets, eager to get them done.

The cabinets were finished on time, and Rusty persuaded Joe to meet him at the Applebys on Saturday morning to install them. It was an easy job so by noon the work was done, and Joe left to go home, but Rusty hung around to visit. Marie offered him a sandwich and salad for lunch, during which she announced to everyone's surprise that she and Cathy were going to town to shop for Cathy a party dress. Cathy had graduated high school with little fanfare and begun studies at the university. She managed to obtain a student job in the library where she came in contact with lots of students, including guys. Several times she had been asked for a date, but she had turned them down because she didn't think she had appropriate clothes. Then a handsome football player invited her to go with him to a party at his frat house. Then, to Rusty's surprise, Marie asked him if he could stay there with Lauren and Ben while they were gone.

"Sure, I'll be happy to," he replied. As soon as they were gone, Lauren began cleaning the kitchen and putting things in the new cabinets, and Rusty wandered into Ben's room to visit. Immediately, Ben said, "All right, Rusty, this is a good time for you to tell me how much you suffered at Angola. I'd like to know what you went through."

"What do you want to know, Ben?"

"Everything. Just start at the beginning."

Rusty was trying hard to forget those five years, but to please Ben, he began. "Ben, it really started before I arrived at Angola. I hated everyone, the investigator on my case, my court-appointed lawyer, the jury, the judge, and the jailer who kept me in jail here while awaiting trial. But, even though I hated them, when the verdict was announced and the sentence pronounced, somehow I felt that I was getting what I deserved. I had been so drunk on the night of the fight that I didn't know whether I was guilty or not, but everyone said I was, so I accepted it that I was and needed to be punished. I'd heard about those 'country-club' prisons and had assumed that I might be sent to one of them.

"Then the judge sentenced me to Angola, the largest maximum security prison in the country. That's where the worst of the worst criminals go. I knew about the violence that existed there, but I didn't know just how bad it was. Most of the prisoners there are in for life, so I couldn't understand why I was being sent there. I thought I knew a little about prison life, but it was a real shock to me. When I arrived I was assigned to a barracks with a dozen other inmates. They initiated me, for sure. But one old black man, named Abraham, took me aside and warned me about who to watch out for, the prison gangs and their leaders, about prisoners killing prisoners, about something akin to prison mafia. Big Mike was the prison boss who bullied everyone. If he told you to give him your lunch, you had better give it, Abraham said.

Abraham, took me aside and warned me of rape. He said, "dey likes white boys; you are fresh meat. Prob'ly tonight dey'll make 'dey move after you go to sleep. It'll be about fo' of 'em, so you can't stop 'em. Three of 'em will hold you down whilst another one rapes you and dey'll take turns. You best be prepared."

"That night an hour after 'lights out' I was lying awake in my bunk, scared of what was sure to happen to me, when they eased up to my bunk and grabbed me. I fought viciously, determined that they would not succeed, but there were too many of them and they were too strong. However, I made enough noise to bring a couple of guards who interrupted the attempt and hauled them off to 'the hole.'"

"What's 'the hole?'" Ben wanted to know.

"It's a cell block where dangerous offenders and troublemakers are placed in individual cells and kept to punish them. The temperature is stifling, and they are permitted out only briefly once a day. It's horrendous."

"Were you ever there?" Ben asked.

"Yes, two times for fighting. I never instigated a fight, but I did try to defend myself."

"Did you just lie around all day?" Ben wanted to know.

"Oh no. Everybody is assigned a job. I was first assigned to the laundry, the worst place in the prison to work. Can you imagine doing dirty, smelly clothes for 7,000 people? There were more than 5,000 prisoners and about 1,800 employees to wash for. Of course there are lots of people who work in the laundry. But trying to get the right clothes back to the right people is a difficult job. I stayed there for about a year.

"Then I was assigned to work in the fields. Angola is an old plantation consisting of 18,000 acres in the bend of the Mississippi River. Sugar cane, vegetables and other things are grown there. Immediately after breakfast we were marched out, usually with hoes, to work all day in the fields. It was hard work, but at least it was outside and it gave me something to keep me busy."

"Were there fences between you and the river?"

"No," he answered. "Though we had armed guards, they didn't worry too much about jail breaks. The river is wide and very deep and covers three sides of the prison. Nobody has managed to escape that way, and the other side is dense forest. Some of the escapees who have gone into those woods full of mosquitos and rattlers have returned to the prison voluntarily. Usually an escapee is caught before he can cross the river. Then after a year in the fields, I was moved to the kitchen, where I washed pots and pans for a year.

"Finally, after they discovered my skills working with wood, I was assigned to the woodworking shop where I stayed until I was released."

"That doesn't seem too bad to me. At least you could see the end of your ordeal. I can't," Ben complained.

"In some ways my experience and yours are similar."

"How do you figure that? You are up walking around after five years. I'm sentenced to life."

"Well," Ben, "the strain of prison is not just physical. Being looked upon as worthless, being ordered around, screamed at, and mistreated by fellow prisoners, and having all your freedom taken away is the hardest. You are told when to go to bed behind locked doors, when to get up, when to eat, and what you can do. That's the hardest part. It's the psychological effect that is the worst in prison. And I think that is your worst problem too."

"How do you figure that?" Ben asked.

"Well, I could say that you don't have to work, you are provided plenty of food, you are cared for, you have a family who loves you, but the emotional effect robs you of happiness.

"Ben, I'd like to tell you what else happened to me at Angola. I was introduced to church and the Bible. I was led to receive Jesus Christ as my Savior. Then I enrolled in the Bible College and finished a four-year degree there. I have new life. What I discovered is that it doesn't matter where you are – in prison or in a wheel chair – you can have life and liberty. It won't get you out of that chair, but it will give you a new heart, forgiveness, and something worth living for."

"Yeah, yeah, I heard you got jailhouse religion."

"Ben I told you about that mighty Mississippi River, but I can tell you there is another river that flows from God. It is mentioned in the Bible: There is a river whose streams make glad the city of God, the holy place where the Most High dwells. God is within her, she will not fall... Psalms(46:4,5). It's a river of His mercy and forgiveness and it brings the Water of Life; that is what Jesus called Himself – the Bread and Water of Life."

"I don't want to hear anything else about it," Ben replied. "You had better go now."

"All right," Ben, "but I'm glad we've had this visit, and I hope we can do it again. Before I go I'd like to ask you one question though. Have you ever considered what responsibility you have for your injuries?"

"What, are you trying to put the blame on me for this?"

"No," Rusty answered, "I just want you to think about it"

In the living room Rusty found Lauren crying. "What's wrong?" he asked.

"Oh nothing. I've just been eavesdropping and it's so sad. I hope Ben is listening." When she had dried her eyes, she asked, "Rusty, is that invitation to church still good?"

"Of course."

"Then I would like to go with you tomorrow. Will it be all right if Cathy and I meet you there?"

"Yes, in fact, you need to be there for Sunday school at 9:45. I'll meet you in front of the church. Okay?"

"I'll be there, and I'll try to bring Cathy."

Rusty was at the church early, Bible and Sunday school book in hand, to meet the girls and lead them into the proper class. To Lauren's surprise, Rusty was taking the place of the regular teacher that day. With confidence he led the group in a lively discussion of the scripture lesson until one of the students, who seemed to have a chip on his shoulder raised a question: "Is it true that you served time in prison for attempted murder?" Lauren was surprised that she was so quick to defend Rusty in her mind and resent the intrusion.

However, Rusty calmly answered, "Yes, that is true. But the term 'attempted murder' suggested that it was what I was trying to do, and that is not true. Unfortunately, some of us were very drunk, so drunk that I don't know what I did, but we got into a brawl and Ben Appleby was seriously injured. By the way, Lauren and Cathy are his sisters. I was accused of the deed and sentenced to Angola where I served five years and I'm grateful, for I was saved there."

Rusty's forthright answer and calm demeanor seemed to shame the questioner and he had no more to say. When the class was over, he exited quickly while several of the group stayed behind to apologize that the subject came up. "Not a problem," Rusty explained.

Pastor Williams delivered a moving message about the peace of God and how He gives it to those who will open their hearts and wills to Him. Lauren seemed truly touched. Rusty felt that it was a message straight from God that fit their needs. When the service was ended, Rusty invited Lauren and Cathy to go to lunch, but they politely declined, saying they needed to go home, so with regrets Rusty bid them goodbye at the front of the church.

Before Rusty could get away a gentleman approached and greeted him, "Hello, Rusty, I'm Lyle. Could I buy you lunch today? My wife had to work and I'm all alone, and it looks like you are too, and I'd like some time to talk with you." It seemed so unusual to Rusty because no one had done so before and because Rusty had not even met the man before. "Let's go get my car and we'll go down to the Chinese buffet if that is okay with you."

"Sure," said Rusty. "It's my favorite place."

Lyle walked with Rusty to a late model Chevrolet and they rode in silence to the restaurant. Once inside, Lyle insisted on paying for the lunches and they filled their plates and found a place to sit in the corner of the dining room. There was little time for conversation as they were eating, until Lyle asked, "How do you like it here, Rusty?"

"I like it. You know I grew up here so I'm familiar with Winslow. I'm glad to be back."

Finished with their meal, over desert and coffee, they visited and talked. Rusty, you probably don't remember me, but I'm Captain Earle with the Winslow Police Department."

"Uh oh," thought Rusty. What could be wrong now? he wondered.

Lyle continued, " I was the detective who investigated the case after the Appleby boy was injured. I also investigated a few other times when you were in trouble with the law. But I want you to know that you are rehabilitated more than any ex-criminal I've ever known, and I'm extremely proud of you."

"Thank you, Sir. I must say that I can't take credit for the changes in my life. It's all because of the Lord in my life that I am a new man now."

"Good. You know that most men who have spent time in prison go right back to their life of crime and soon wind up back in. But I am convinced that it will not happen to you."

"Thank you, Sir. So am I. I can't believe that I once lived the life that I did."

"Rusty, I'm just curious. Why did you come back here where you would not be readily accepted, where your old wild friends are, and where some of your victims still live?"

"Lyle, when I was being released from Angola, the warden said to me, 'Now go and mend your fences,' so that's what I'm trying to do because I also believe that is what the Lord would have me do. I'm doing everything I can to help the Appleby family and gain their forgiveness."

"That's very commendable. I hear that it hasn't been easy."

"That's right, but we're making progress."

"Let me tell you something, Rusty. As I investigated the crime done in that barroom my gut feeling was that you didn't do it. But the only witness who would come forward to finger you swore that you swung the chair that hit Appleby. That was the mayor's son, Richard. With no other evidence, all I could do was present what I had to the grand jury and because of your reputation they were quick to charge you. Then your appointed defense attorney didn't help you, so the petit jury found you guilty and the judge sentenced you to the maximum. Did you hit the boy?"

"Lyle," Rusty said, "I have no recollection of hitting him, but I was so drunk that I don't remember what happened."

"Well, if you were not guilty, I'm just sorry that you had to go to prison."

"This may sound stupid, Lyle, but I'm glad I went to prison. It was there that I went to church for the first time in my life. For the first time in my life someone told me about the Lord and how to be saved. It was there that I was saved, and there that I went to Bible college and graduated with honors. That wouldn't have happened to me if I had not been there."

"That's commendable, Rusty. I'm proud of you."

"Lyle, I'm not arguing with the verdict, but I am curious about the case. Do you, by chance, still have the reports from the investigation?"

"I'm sure we do, but since it was closed so long ago, I don't know if I can find them. If you would like, I'll see what I can do."

"Would you please?"

"Yes, I will and I'll let you know. Well, I need to go now, so I'll drive you back to the church."

"Thank you, but if you don't mind, it is such a pretty day, I'd like to walk."

"Okay, I'll see you soon then."

"Thanks for lunch," Rusty called as they walked away.

Rusty didn't know what, if anything, would be gained by studying the investigator's report, yet he felt drawn to it. He had a desire to know as much about the incident as possible, even though he would still be grateful for the Angola experience.

Chapter 13

SUCCESS IS SWEET

Clark's wife, suffering from Parkinson's Disease, was having balance problems, and when she climbed onto a kitchen stepstool to change a light bulb, she lost her balance and fell to the floor and broke her hip. Two hours passed before Clark found her there, and he blamed himself for not being there with her. She was hospitalized for a few days, and Clark stayed with her even after she came home. Although he called and told Rusty what had happened and he shared it with the other men, they didn't see Clark for weeks. Then when he came to the shop again, he called Rusty into the office.

"Rusty, I'm going to spend more time with my wife through the rest of her life. I hope she will live for years, but she will need constant companionship and I intend to provide it. So since I'm not going to be involved in the operation of the business and more responsibility will be placed on your shoulders, I think we should speed up our schedule for you to buy it."

"Listen, Clark," Rusty responded, "we will continue the work here as always. You don't have to sell."

"I know, and I appreciate that, but I think I just need to relieve myself of any responsibility here and devote my time to my wife, so let's talk about some terms."

"Clark, you know that I have very little money and I don't know if I can get the financing."

"I know," Clark continued, "but let me tell you what I have in mind. I will sell you 51% of the business and I will be a silent partner. I will want you to pay me $100,000 for which you will pay me regular payments from the proceeds of the business. Then after the payments and the overhead are paid, I'll get one-half of the profits of the business, payable at the end of the year. That means that you would not have to have upfront money and I will finance the loan. How does that sound?"

"Clark, I haven't had much business experience, but that sounds mighty charitable to me. It sounds like the business will be paying for itself."

"Exactly. That's the way I want it," Clark said. "However, we will have to have a lawyer involved and maybe a banker and an accountant, so I want you to pick those out and go to them and talk about the kind of transaction I'm proposing and let them advise you."

"Clark, I trust you completely, so if you have those three who do business with you now, I would just like to continue to use them."

"Okay, then, you just take some time and go talk to them; then we will talk about this some more."

The next day Rusty came to work in dress clothes, surprising the crew, so he told them he had some personal business to see about and for them to continue their assigned projects and he would be back by noon. The names Clark gave Rusty were Mr. Wilson at First City Bank, the ABC accounting firm, and Attorney Dale Albertson. Without any appointments, Rusty began making the rounds. Mr. Albertson had high praise for Clark and his offer. Mrs. Johnson at ABC confirmed that Clark's Woodworking was on solid ground financially, always showing a profit and that the offer would be good for Rusty. Finally, the bank Manager, Mr. Wilson, said, "Other than handling Clark's accounts I've had very little dealings with him. He hasn't needed a loan in years and his balance is substantial. "Young man, I think you are being offered a gold mine with little risk to you. Go for it."

Rusty went to Clark's home the next day to tell him what he found and his response. He found Mrs. Howie in bed but in good spirits. "Rusty," she said, "Clark has discussed his offer to you with me, and I'm very pleased with it. I can't think of anyone I would want to sell the business to more than you. You're just a shining example of what Jesus can do for a man."

"Thank you, Mrs. Howie."

"Just call me Eva. I hope this doesn't mean that you will stop coming by to see us."

"Oh, no, M….I mean Eva."

"There is something else, Rusty," she said. "I hear that you are seeing that Appleby girl, Lauren, isn't she? I'm so glad. She comes from a good family. It's unfortunate what has happened to that family, but she will come out of this stronger than ever."

"Thank you. I think so too."

Moving to Clark's office, Rusty said, "Clark, I've talked with all of these people and found them all agreeing that the business is solid and that your offer is generous, so if you are sure you are not cheating yourself, I'll accept your terms."

"Great," responded Clark. "I'll talk with the attorney tomorrow and have him start the paper work. And, Rusty, I would like to come to talk to the men. How about if I have lunch catered Friday and come eat with you and talk? There's a fish place across town that caters, and the food is good."

"That sounds great. I'll tell them not to bring their lunches." Excusing himself, Rusty left and went immediately to share the news with Lauren. As they talked he shared his dreams for the future, including marriage and a family. Though he stopped short of proposing, she thought he was hinting at it and she could be interested.

At 11:30 the next Friday morning Clark showed up at the shop and began setting up tables for the lunch, scheduled to arrive at 12. He went around chatting with each of the employees in his usually way of making everyone feel special. Then when the food arrived and was spread on the tables, Clark asked Rusty to offer thanks, and he asked God to bless Mr. and Mrs. Howie and the men, then thanked God for the food.

They enjoyed a little banter and teasing of Rusty about his love life as they ate. But when the meal was finished, they all wanted to know about Mrs. Howie's condition and offered to help anyway they could. Clark thanked them, then began his talk. "Men, I appreciate every one of you. We've been together for a long time, and I trust all of you completely. You've become like family to me. Thank you for your loyalty and your excellent work. You've made this business the success it is today.

"Now, I'm afraid it's time for me to give it up."

"You're not closing it down are you, Boss?"

"No, I'm not. That's why I want to talk to you. My wife's health is such that I need to be with her all of the time, and I'm at retirement age, so I'm selling Clark's Woodworking."

"Oh me," Joe responded. "I hope it will be to someone who will keep us on and that we can get along with as we have with you."

"Well, I think it is," Clark continued. "I'm selling to Rusty. He has been here and done a good job for a few years, and he is the foreman now, so you already know what it will be like to work for him. Frankly, he has become like a son to me. You know that my wife and I could never have children, and Rusty has no living parents, so I feel like we are father and son." Tears rolled down Rusty's cheeks for he had never heard Clark speak of him in that way.

"The papers are being drawn up now, so we should be closing the deal in a couple of weeks," Clark continued. "I want you all to know that this decision is not intended to offend any one of you, and I hope you will be as loyal as you've always been, and that you can continue with the same kind of camaraderie we've always enjoyed. Do you have any questions?"

"No questions, just regrets that you won't be here anymore."

"Well, to tell you the truth, I'm selling Rusty just 51% of the business, so I'll still be part owner, so if he gets out of line I'll be around to straighten him out."

"Oh, I think there is someone else in the wings who'll do that," Joe replied.

With that, Clark excused himself, saying, "I have just a few personal things I want to get from the office, and I'm sure Rusty has some things to say to you before he sends you back to slaving."

Rusty did and he assured them that their jobs were intact, and promised that things would continue as they had been. "If it isn't broke, don't fix it," he said. "You all know about my past, and you don't seem to have judged me for that. To be honest, I'm as shocked about this as you must be. To be accepted by Clark, you, and many others, has been beyond my wildest dreams. You also know that I'm a Christian, having been saved while in prison. I will try not to flout my Christianity, but I do want it to show because it should. So I want it to be foremost in my work and personal relationships. I believe I am right in thinking that all of you go to church pretty regularly and I'm glad of it. Now if you have no objections, I will begin something new. When we come to work on Monday morning, I want us to gather for fifteen minutes to read the Bible and pray. Don't fret, you will be on the clock. Then when we stop to eat lunch, if possible let's eat together and begin our meals with a prayer of thanks. You see, I believe that God is to be a part of everything in our lives, including work. He has done so much for me and just worked miracles in my life since I was saved. I can't thank Him enough. Any questions?"

"No, 'Boss,'" they responded.

"Then if we want to get paid at the end of the week, let's get back to work."

There seemed to be an air of excitement among the men, and a new devotion to their work in the coming weeks because they felt secure and weren't worried about what Clark would do with the business. To a man every one of the crew expressed appreciation to Rusty for his decisions. Like Rusty, they could not understand how an ex-con could possibly buy a large, successful business, and Rusty didn't tell them. "It's all in God's hands," he would say.

Once the papers were signed and it was decided to leave the company name as it was, work continued as usual. Most people outside of the business didn't even know about the transfer. Rusty took a little teasing for having "church" on Mondays, but they didn't mind attending on company time. In fact, Sammy said jokingly, "If they will pay me my hourly wage for it I'll be in church every Sunday." Rusty took it all in stride, and everyone enjoyed the group lunch time together. Rusty used that time to answer any questions about his faith. Of course, they always asked when he would be saying "I do."

Chapter 14

GROWING TRUST

When Rusty's phone rang, waking him from a deep sleep, he looked at the clock which showed 11:00 and wondered who would be calling him. "Hello," he said. All he could hear was the sniffling of someone crying on the line. "May I help you?" he asked.

"Is this Rusty?" she asked.

"Yes."

"Rusty, this is Cathy. I need a ride home, and Mom's at work in our van."

"Where are you?"

"At a frat house at the university."

"Are you okay? What are you doing there?"

"I came here to a party. I'm okay, but I need a ride. Can you come get me?"

"Which house is it?" he asked.

"The first one of Frat Row."

"I'll be there is ten minutes. Where can I find you when I get there?"

"I'm in the bathroom. Come near the door and I'll be watching for you."

Dressing hurriedly, Rusty drove to the school, found the house and went in search of the bathroom. As he approached the door, Cathy emerged, wearing her lovely party dress. She ran to Rusty and grabbed his arm and held on tightly as if she were afraid. He didn't ask what the problem was because he thought she would volunteer it later if she wanted to. As they

88

walked through the crowd, a large boy, dressed in his tuxedo, smelling of alcohol, stepped in front of him and demanded, "Hey, Dude, where do you think you are going with my girl?"

"I'm taking her home, step aside," Rusty replied.

"You may think you are, but I brought her here and I'm taking her home when I'm done with her" he bristled, raising his fists to fight. In a flash, Rusty grabbed him and put him in a headlock and held him until he begged to be released.

By that time other students had gathered around to separate them. Rusty released him and started for the door again with Cathy still clinging to him when someone asked, "Cathy, do you know this man?"

"Yes, this is Rusty Jenson. He is my sister's boyfriend and my friend. I called him to come take me home because my date was trying to force me to go upstairs with him. I'm leaving with him right now." They parted and allowed them to pass through the group, out the door, and to the truck.

As Rusty drove, Cathy was crying softly. "I'm sorry, Cathy, that you had this bad experience."

"Experience!" She responded. "That's just the problem. I've had no experience. I've never dated and didn't know what I was getting into. I fell for the first football hero who showed up and asked me out. He had no interest in me except for a bedroom partner. It'll be a long time before I'll trust another man."

"Now, Cathy, you can't judge all men by one jerk."

"I know," she confessed, "and I do trust you."

When Cathy and Rusty knocked on the door and Lauren answered, she was surprised to see Rusty bringing Cathy home. Her date was supposed to bring her home. "What's wrong?" she asked. Cathy fell into her arms, crying. "Now don't cry, Cathy. Come sit down and tell me what happened."

"I was such a fool," Cathy explained. "I accepted a date with a man because he is handsome and a football star. And I went to a Frat House party without knowing what could happen to me there."

"I know. I've never been to one, but I've heard some of the students talking about their parties."

When Marie came bursting into the room, and saw them all sitting at the table drinking hot chocolate, she demanded, "What's wrong? What are you doing here at this hour, Rusty?"

"Mom," Lauren rushed to his defense. "He just drove Cathy home."

"Cathy, did he do something to you?"

"No, no, Mom. He rescued me." Then she had to repeat the whole story to Marie.

"I didn't know you were going to a party at a Frat House, Cathy. Those can be pretty wild. You weren't hurt were you?"

"No, Mom. But I don't know what might have happened if I had not been able to call Rusty."

"I guess I should apologize and thank you, Rusty," Marie said.

When everyone was calmed down and Rusty was preparing to leave, he said, "I have a suggestion. Tell me what you think about it. Suppose we get Ben into the van Saturday and all of us go to the lake. We could grill hamburgers."

Both Cathy and Lauren thought it was a wonderful idea, but Marie could see only the potential problems. "How could we get him into the van?"

"I can build a little ramp with some ¾ inch plywood," Rusty answered. "It will hold his weight and the chair, and it will be light enough that I can handle it. I may have to go in the truck to haul the grill and the ramp, but that's okay."

"If the weather is pretty, we can try it," Lauren agreed. "What time?"

"Okay," Marie conceded, "but you know we will all have to help."

"Oh we will," they promised.

With that settled, Rusty left the house, but Lauren followed him outside. "Thank you, Rusty," she said," for rescuing Cathy and for the offer to take us to the lake." With that she reached up and kissed him on the cheek. "Now I'll get to spend time with you Saturday and Sunday. Good night." Rusty floated back to town, savoring that first kiss and making plans for the outing.

Saturday was a warm spring day for the trip to the lake. Rusty had fashioned a ramp that would create an incline for Ben to guide his chair up and into the van. And he had removed the middle seat for him, yet it was still a tight fit. Furthermore, Ben's head rubbed the roof. Cathy sat in the back to be with Ben, but Lauren chose to ride in the truck with Ben. The trip was uneventful, and the ramp worked beautifully, but Ben had trouble navigating the chair in the sand, so Rusty helped him to a spot in the shade and set up the grill nearby. Being only a short distance from the water, the girls tried their hand at fishing.

"I remember when Dad used to bring us fishing here," Lauren said. "We never caught anything but it was fun anyway. I miss those times with Dad, but I can't forgive him for what he has done to all of us."

"Do you think he will ever come back, Lauren?"

"I'm afraid not. He has someone else in his life now, and it's like he has disowned us."

Since the fish weren't biting, Cathy and Lauren took a stroll along the shore. Cathy said, "Lauren, I was so traumatized by my one date that I don't know if I can ever date again. I want to, but I'm afraid."

"Just give it some time, Cathy, and then be very careful about who you go with. There are some gentlemen, like Rusty, left out there."

"But where do I find them?" Cathy wanted to know.

"You know that we're going to church with Rusty now. That might be a good place to look. I know that Rusty's faith is what makes him a good man. And I'm sure there are others like him."

"Lauren, do love Rusty?"

"I'm not sure, but I think I do."

"How do you know?"

"It's hard to explain, but when I can't wait to see him, and I want to be with him all of the time and to please him even more than myself, I think that tells me something. I can't explain it, but I think you just know."

"Do you plan to marry him?"

"He hasn't asked me, but he has hinted at it. I want to marry, but I have to think of Ben and Mom. I can't just leave them. We will just have to see how things work out, I guess."

The car horn was blowing and Rusty called out, "lunch time," so the girls started back to the picnic site. Rusty had brought lawn chairs, and plenty of food: soft drinks, chips, etc. and he had grilled the burgers. He laid out all of the fixings on the tailgate of his truck and invited them to dress their burgers to suit themselves. Marie fixed Ben's and cut it into small pieces to feed him and he drank from a straw.

"This is good," Rusty. "Where did you learn to cook?" Marie asked.

"In prison," he quipped, and Ben laughed for the first time in ages.

"I like this," Lauren said. "I'm glad I thought of it."

"You thought of it? What do you mean?" Cathy jumped to Rusty's defense.

Mom brought up the subject of all the changes that were in the making for them. Lauren would graduate as a nurse soon. Cathy was half through college. She feared that she and Ben would be left alone soon and she couldn't figure out how they could make it.

"Don't worry about it, Mom," Lauren offered. "I'm going to find a job in Winslow and I believe my pay will support this family. I want you to be able to quit that job you despise. We're still going to be together, I promise."

"Now, Lauren, you can't sacrifice your future for us," Marie objected. "We will work something out."

"I know we will," Lauren responded.

Rusty chimed in, "You know that I believe strongly in that promise of God that He will provide. We may not know what's in the future, but He does."

"I wish I could have your faith, Rusty, but I don't. Where has God been during the last few years? Goodness knows, I prayed for miracles," Marie replied.

"You know, Mom," Lauren said, "some pretty miraculous things have happened to us in these last years. Maybe God has answered our prayers in ways we didn't recognize." Without voicing it, Lauren was thinking of all that Rusty was doing for them.

By mid-afternoon, Ben was looking sunburned and exhausted so, over his objections, Rusty loaded him into the van, cleaned up their picnic site, and they headed home. It was a breeze to get Ben out of the van and back into the house. Then when everyone was thanking Rusty for the outing, to everybody's surprise, Ben said, "Yea, Ben, thank you."

Chapter 15

NEW REVELATIONS

When Rusty came for the girls Sunday morning, they came out looking beautiful in their nicest dresses. After going in to speak to Ben, Rusty came back and asked Marie, "Mrs. Appleby, may I escort these lovely ladies to church and lunch today?"

"It looks like they are old enough to decide for themselves," she answered.

"Would you like for us to bring lunch for you and Ben?" he asked.

"Oh no, I'll fix us something."

The worship service began with joyous congregational singing. It felt to Lauren and Cathy that the people enjoyed being there. Rusty was even called on to pray in the service. True to his nature, he prayed a very mature prayer, even thanking God for the experiences in his life that brought him to Christ. When the service was ended, people hugged each other and chatted, and Captain Lyle came to Rusty and said, "I have something for you in the car. Wait for me out front and I'll get it."

In just a few minutes, he came back with a fat folder, and when he gave it to Rusty, he said, "This is just a copy, but I can't afford to let it out, so be sure to return it to me." Rusty tucked the folder under his arm and walked with the girls to the truck. As they drove to the restaurant, Lauren asked, "Wasn't that the police captain Lyle Earle who gave you something?"

"Yes, it was."

"May I ask what it was? I'm just curious," Lauren said.

"I guess it won't hurt to tell you that it is the investigator's report from that barroom brawl."

"Why did he give it to you?" she asked.

"I asked him for it because I want to know more about what happened to send me to prison. I was so drunk I don't remember anything about it."

"May we take it in and look at it at lunch?" Cathy asked. "I'm curious too."

"I guess," Rusty consented, "if you promise not to tell anyone."

They were seated in a secluded area of the restaurant, and soon a delicious plate of home-cooked food was served to them. "It's been so long since we've been out to eat," commented Cathy. "I can hardly remember when."

By the time they finished the meal the crowd had dwindled so much that they felt all alone. Rusty asked the waitress if they could sit awhile and drink tea while they looked over some papers. With her consent, he opened the folder and they began to peruse its contents. "There is so much here it's like looking for a needle in a haystack," Cathy said. "What are we looking for anyway?"

"Anything of importance - witnesses, testimony, names, items of evidence"- Rusty responded. Then he divided the papers among them so the work would go faster. He found the testimony of the bartender who said there were five or six people involved in the brawl but most scattered when they heard the siren coming. Only Rusty, Ben, and Richard Overstreet, the mayor's son, were left in the bar when the police arrived. "That isn't much help," Rusty complained.

"Look, here is something," Lauren said. "It says here that both the bartender and Richard testified that Ben started the fight. I wonder if he knows that. I can't wait to get home and ask him."

"Could I ask you not to do that?" Rusty asked. " Ben doesn't have any memory of what happened, but I think he is beginning to remember some things. You know he is having those flashbacks. I would rather he remembered that instead us bringing the accusation to him. Let's give him time to discover it. Okay?"

"That's wise. Thank you, Rusty."

"It says here that Richard Overstreet was the only one who testified that he saw you hit Ben. Do you think we could talk to him?" Cathy asked.

"No," answered Lauren. "he was killed in a drug deal gone bad a few years ago."

They stuffed the papers back into the folder and started toward home, where they found both Marie and Ben taking an afternoon nap, so Rusty left the girls and drove away as quietly as possible. Back at home, he spent the rest of the afternoon studying the investigative report. However, the only witness to identify him as the guilty one was the mayor's son. Even the bartender claimed he didn't see who hit Ben with the chair. Rusty didn't understand why, but something about the report still bugged him.

Lauren's graduation was approaching and the TLC Nursing Home administrator had already asked her to come on board as the head nurse. Lauren loved the fact that she felt she was helping people who really needed her there, so she was willing to accept, despite the long hours and hard work. Many of the senior patients had no one to visit them regularly and she felt she could bring a little cheer into their lives. She loved them, and they loved her in turn. The pay would be equal to that she could get elsewhere, so she agreed to begin the week after graduation.

Rusty was debating what he could do for Lauren's graduation when he talked to Mrs. Howie. After he shared his dilemma with her, she said, "Rusty do you love that girl?"

"Yes, I do," he answered.

"Then ask her to marry you and give her a ring."

"Do you actually think she would marry an ex-con and be stuck with me for the rest of her life?"

"Look, I've heard enough of this 'ex-con' business. Stop putting yourself down. You are as good and honorably as any man I know, so think better of yourself. And I'll tell you, when I've seen you two together I know she cares deeply for you. Go for it. The worst she can say is 'no.'"

With her advice ringing in his head, Rusty went to the local jewelry store to shop for a ring, and he chose the biggest ring he thought he could afford. Still uncertain, he asked the owner, "If she turns me down, will you take the ring back and refund my money?" He assured Rusty that he would but also encouraged him to think positive.

On the night of graduation Rusty hired Sarah, the home health nurse, who had attended Ben to come stay with him while the family went to the graduation. He would have taken Ben too, but Ben didn't want others to see him handicapped. So Marie, Cathy, and Lauren drove to the university, and Rusty met them there with the ring in his pocket. After a long graduation speech with all the preliminaries, the time came for Lauren to walk across the stage. She was graduating with honors and they were so proud of her. Tears rolled down Marie's cheeks as she watched, but Rusty and Cathy clapped loudly. After a time of visiting and congratulations, Rusty invited them all to the fanciest restaurant in town for dinner, but Marie declined, saying that she and Cathy would just grab a burger and go home to relieve Sarah, so that left Rusty with the perfect opportunity to propose.

As Rusty and Lauren dined on lobster tail with all of the trimmings, he seemed very nervous. Lauren noticed it and asked, "Is something wrong, Rusty? You seem very quiet and maybe nervous."

"Well, if you must know," he began, "I am very nervous because I need to say something very important. Lauren, I love you," he blurted out, "and I'm asking you to be my wife. Now you can think about it for a while because I know that I'm not the best candidate for a husband, and I wouldn't want you to make a mistake. I believe it would be a marriage for the rest of our lives."

Lauren reached over and touched his lips and said, "Hush, Rusty. Yes, I accept. I love you too and I'll be delighted to be your wife for life."

"What?" he asked loudly. "I can hardly believe it. That makes me so happy." With that he rose from his seat and knelt before her and slipped the ring on her finger.

"Rusty, people are watching," Lauren said.

"I don't care. Here, I'll tell them all. Hey everybody, Lauren Appleby is going to be my wife and you're all invited to the wedding." Everyone joined in the clapping, and Lauren stood and bowed politely. She was a princess to Rusty. Arm in arm they glided from the restaurant and to the truck where they shared more kisses than ever before. "I'm so happy, Lauren. Thank you. When can we get married?"

"Rusty, you know that I still have Mom and Ben to think about. I'll have to help care for him, and I intend to support them financially. With my working, Mom will need to be with Ben more, so I'm going to insist that she quit her job; therefore, I don't know how soon I can leave home."

Rusty assured her that he understood and that he would provide whatever help he could, and that he would wait for her as long as necessary. After all, there were still issues with Ben that he hoped to resolve. When they drove up to the Appleby home, Rusty jumped out, came around and opened the door for Lauren and dragged her into the house where he announced, "Hey, everybody, Lauren has agreed to marry me." Lauren showed the lovely ring and they marveled at it, after which Marie congratulated them and gave her blessing to the wedding and hugged both of them.

Rusty went in to see Ben who was asleep, but Rusty woke him to tell him the news. "Did you wake me up just to tell me that?" he grumbled. "It could have waited until tomorrow or next week, for that matter. Rusty, I'm glad. You and Lauren are a good match. Sit down and let's talk a little. Just what did you mean when you asked if I had considered that I had a part in my injuries?"

"Well, Ben, I just thought that since you were involved in the fight that you should recognize your responsibility. I'm not trying to place all of the blame on you, but I just want you to think about it."

"To tell you the truth," Rusty, "I haven't been able to remember anything about it. I guess either I was too drunk or I just wanted to block it out of my mind. But here lately I've been having some flashbacks and what I've seen is disturbing. I think I must have started the fight."

Rusty told him then about the police report and that it confirmed the fact. "So, ultimately, I'm as much to blame, Rusty, as you are, and here I've been blaming you for all of it. If I hadn't wanted to fight and started it there might not have been a fight."

"Ben," Rusty responded, "that's not important. I'm just sorry that you got hurt. Do you happen to remember who all was involved?"

"No, not really. But I know Richard, and three or four more. Richard's dead and the rest are probably dead or in jail somewhere. But if I remember more, I'll tell you."

"Thanks for telling me, Ben. I'll be going now. Goodnight." Lauren followed Rusty out to the truck for a goodnight kiss. They were both as happy as they could be.

As he drove home, Rusty thought about what Ben had discovered and felt good that he accepted responsibility. But there was more that he couldn't quiet put his finger on. What was it? "Not now," he said aloud. "Maybe later. For now I'm going home and start my bucket list."

At home, Rusty prayed that God would direct him to the important things to be his goals in the coming months. He got paper and pencil and as a thought came to him, he wrote it down.

See Lauren saved and a member of the church

1. Buy a new car for Lauren to use
2. Buy land on which to build a house
3. See all of the Applebys saved and in church
4. Keep Clark's Woodworking going strong
5. Get married

With the list complete, at least for the present, Rusty prayed again thanking God for guiding him. He prayed that all he planned was in God's will for him and if not that God would show him. Then he confessed that he didn't know how to accomplish his goals and asked for God's help.

With that he went to bed and slept soundly. Arising early the next morning, he left to go see Clark and Eva and tell them the good news. He knew that they were always up early and were probably drinking coffee. He sure would like a cup because he hadn't taken the time to brew his own. And, just as he thought, their light was own and Clark opened the door even before he knocked. "Good morning early bird. Come in and have some coffee. I hope you aren't the bearer of bad news."

"On the contrary," Clark began. "I have good news. Lauren and I are engaged."

"Wonderful," Eva spoke from the kitchen. "I just knew that it would happen and it makes me very happy."

"When is the big event?" Clark inquired.

"Well, we haven't set a date yet. You know Lauren has to help her mother with Ben, and she has taken the job as head nurse at the nursing home, so she can't just walk out on her mother."

"My, that sounds like a long-term problem," Eva said.

"I'm working on it," Rusty replied. "I've made a list of goals for the next year or so. Of course one of them is to keep the business strong,

Another is to purchase some land and to start planning for a house that will accommodate Lauren and her family. I want it to have an apartment for Marie and Ben. After the house is finished we can move the family in and we can be married."

"That's mighty big of you, Rusty," Clark said. "Do you have a spot in mind to buy?"

"Not yet, but I'm on the lookout for some."

Rusty, it just so happens that we own a two-acre lot about a mile from the shop. Eva and I had thought that we might build there some day but never got around to it. If you think you might be interested in it, I'll be glad to show it to you." That sounded good to Rusty so they planned to meet at the shop at lunch and drive out to see the land.

At noon, Clark showed up with his lunch and sat with the crew and ate, recalling old times. He asked about their families and about what was going on in their lives, and answered their questions about Eva and whether he was enjoying retirement. Then Clark and Rusty drove the mile to the site which was on a slight knoll declining to a small creek on the backside. It looked ideal to Rusty, so he asked the price.

"Look, Rusty," Clark said. "You've become like a son to me, so even though the land values have increased significantly, I'll sell you this place for your home for the same as I paid for it twenty years ago, and I'll finance it for you. We'll just add it to that note you are paying on the business. How does that sound?"

Rusty couldn't believe Clark's generosity and told him it was too good of a deal to pass up. "But I don't want to cheat you, Clark."

"Look, Son," Clark responded, "we have done well through the years and invested wisely in real estate. Eva and I will never need all that we have accumulated, so I'm delighted to help you. I'll just be sharing a bit in all the generous things you are doing. If you would like, I'll get the transfer of title started this week."

"That's great."

Back at the shop, Clark went home to be with Eva, and Rusty went into the office, closed the door and thanked God for His provisions. "I know now that this is your will, Lord," he prayed. The men wondered what had transpired for they could tell by the expression on Rusty's face that it was good, but none asked.

Rusty showed up at Lauren's that evening with his Bible in hand, and she knew what the discussion would be about. God and His Word were so important to Rusty and she wanted to share that love and commitment. After their greetings and a kiss, Rusty went to speak to Ben in his room. Cathy was in her bedroom studying for a test, so he and Lauren sat at the kitchen table with the open Bible before them and Rusty began to discuss her relationship with the Lord. In answer to his question, Lauren said, "Rusty, I have hoped we could talk about this for some time. After seeing what Christ has done in your life, I want to have what you have. I believe in God, but I've never really known how to have Him in my life. Can you tell me?"

Carefully, Rusty led her through the scriptures that tell why one needs Christ and how He offers Himself to us and invites us to come to Him in faith and receive salvation. Then, before he could even ask, Lauren asked, "Can I do that now even though we are not in church?" With that they bowed their heads and held hands and Rusty led her to pray for salvation. Both faces beamed afterward.

Rusty said, "I'm so proud of you. Now we can be equally joined together. Let me show you what the Bible says: 'Be ye not unequally yoked together with unbelievers: for what fellowship hath righteousness with unrighteousness? And what communion hath light with darkness'" (II Corinthians 6:14).

"Does that mean that you wouldn't have married me, an unbeliever, unrighteous, and in the dark?" Lauren chided.

"I don't have to answer that now, do I?"

"Cathy has been going to church with us and I think she is interested too. Will you tell her?"

"Lauren," Rusty replied, "one of the first steps for a new Christian is to learn to tell others about your new life and to lead others to trust Christ too. So why don't I show you how and you lead Cathy to Christ?

"Okay, I guess. I'm just afraid I might mess it up."

"Not if you are sincere and use the scriptures I show you."

"By the way," Rusty changed the subject, "will you keep your Saturday morning open so you can go shopping with me?"

"Yes, I will, but what are we shopping for?"

"You'll find out Saturday." With that Rusty got his goodnight kiss and headed home. He thanked the Lord again for another goal met. "This is just too good to be true. Only God could do this. Help me, Lord, for I know that Satan will exert himself in our lives some way soon. Everything is going too well to suit the wily one. Please, Lord, I'll need your power when it comes."

Chapter 16

LOVE TESTED

Saturday morning Rusty picked Lauren up early, even before she had eaten breakfast, because he couldn't wait to show her the house site. He promised they would eat in town, but when he drove through town and out past the shop, she was confused. Then he turned off the road onto the land he had purchased and said, "Welcome to your new home site."

"What do you mean?" she asked.

"You know I intend to build us a house, so I bought this lot from Clark on which to build it. It's perfect, near the shop, and close to town. It will be ideal for us, don't you think?"

"It's a lovely setting, Rusty. I can't believe that you were able to find such a good place so quickly or that you are moving so fast toward building a house when we aren't even married yet." She did admire the place. It was ideally situated, but secretly she resented the fact that Rusty had made the choice for their home without even consulting her, and that he already had plans for the house. Would she be able to have any input in its design, she wondered. Even though she knew that Rusty meant well, she still felt left out, but she couldn't bring herself to tell him yet.

Rusty chose IHOP for a breakfast of pancakes. Again, Lauren felt that she had no part in the decision. Over breakfast, Lauren told her fiancée that she had witnessed to Cathy the night before and that Cathy had prayed to receive Christ and how happy it made her to know that she was able to lead someone else to Christ, and that Cathy had been saved. "What should we do now about joining the church?" she asked.

"Well, Sunday when the final hymn of invitation is being sung you just walk down the aisle and tell the pastor that you have been saved and that you want to publicly profess Christ and follow Him in baptism and church membership. He'll probably pray with you, then tell the congregation your decision. Maybe Cathy will come with you."

"Good. We will do it tomorrow."

Having stuffed themselves with pancakes and sausage, washed down with black coffee, they set out to shop. What are we looking for, Lauren wondered but didn't ask. When Rusty drove into a car dealership, she had the answer. "Why are we here?" she asked.

"You know I'm always driving the company truck because I have no car. I can't possibly take my bride on a honeymoon trip in a truck, so I'm going to buy a car."

"But Rusty," she protested, "it's going to be a while before we will need it for that. Besides I can ride in a truck. I did it this morning."

"Let's look, anyway." Then Rusty walked directly to a Chevrolet Malibu which Lauren felt he must have already picked out. It was to be his car, after all, why shouldn't he pick it out? She couldn't help but wonder why he wanted her along, however. Wouldn't the car belong to both of them after the wedding? Yet she had no say in the choice. Then, she caught herself and scolded herself for resenting Rusty's leadership and decision making. After all, wouldn't he be the head of their house? She knew she must put a stop to this attitude.

They took the car for a test drive and came back to the dealership where Rusty made the down payment and signed the papers. Then he surprised Lauren by handing her the keys. "Your schedule conflicts with Cathy's so you need a car to drive yourself to work. You will have it broke in by the time we need it." Lauren felt so ashamed of her hurt feelings when all Rusty was doing was thinking of her, and she began to cry. "You are too good to me, Rusty."

Rusty mentally marked one more thing off his bucket list as he followed her in his truck to her home and into the driveway where she blew the horn to get everyone's attention. Marie and Cathy came out to inspect the new car and hear all about it, while Ben watched out of the window.

When in the house Rusty congratulated Cathy on her recent experience and called her his sister in the Lord, and told her that before long she would be his sister twice. Ben seemed disturbed when Rusty went to his room to visit. "What's wrong, Ben?" he asked.

"I don't know if I want to tell you, Rusty."

"Why? You know you can tell me anything."

Tearfully, Ben began, "I think I have to apologize to you. I had another flashback, and I saw more about the fight we had, and it was not you who hit me. I saw Richard coming at me with the uplifted chair swinging it, and then everything went black." Rusty was stunned. For more than ten years now he had lived with the guilt of paralyzing Ben. If, in fact, he didn't do it, why was he accused? Oh, he remembered, It was Richard's testimony that caused it, and all the time, he was the guilty one, and now he is dead.

"Ben, I'm shocked, wondering what might have been if I hadn't been charged, convicted, and incarcerated. Are you sure that this is the straight of it?"

"As sure as I've ever been sure of anything," Ben replied. "Here I've been blaming you and hating you when you aren't guilty. Now you don't have to feel guilty anymore, and you don't have to try so hard to pay for your wrong. You'll probably be able to forget me, all of us now, even Lauren."

"What are you talking about, Ben? I admit that at first I was trying to make amends, which I didn't even have to do. But, listen, I love Lauren and intend to marry her. I also care about you, and I'm going to continue to do as much for you and your family as possible. When Lauren and I marry your family will be mine, all the family I have." By that time Ben was boohooing, attracting the attention of the women, who rushed into the room concerned about the problem. Ben was crying so, he simply said, "Rusty will have to tell you later." So, later, when Ben had settled, Rusty sat with the ladies in the living room and told the story and assured them that he would continue to assist them in any way he could, even though he thought he was absolved from guilt.

"I'm glad to hear that, Rusty," Marie said. "As hard as I try I don't think I would have ever forgiven you completely. Now I don't have to."

Early Sunday morning Rusty called to see if Lauren wanted him to pick them up for church. "No, silly, Lauren responded. We have wheels. In fact, you be ready at 9:30 and we will pick you up. Don't be late, now." And, as promised they pulled up at exactly 9:30 and headed to church in time for Sunday school. Then came the worship service and before the pastor's message based on Psalms 32, about the joy of being forgiven, a quartet sang "There is a River," and Rusty thought about a river, not the Mississippi, but a deep river that flowed from God bringing to him the Water of life and still flowed through him. He was comforted by the promise that it had no end. Rusty felt that both the hymn and the sermon fit the occasion.

When the invitation was given, Rusty walked down the aisle with Lauren and Cathy hand-in-hand to make their profession of faith in Christ. Rusty couldn't hold back the tears of happiness, and all the church family expressed delight that the two Appleby girls had done something their parents never had. Plans were made with the pastor for their baptism the next Sunday morning, and Rusty began planning to provide a way for Marie to be present. The girls went to lunch with Rusty and then for an afternoon drive in the new car. Rusty and Lauren drove Cathy to see their future home site for he was so proud of it, but he still didn't realize that Lauren felt left out.

Sunday was not a work day, so Rusty could stay and visit with Lauren's family until evening. They brought Ben out onto the front porch and they enjoyed lemonade in the sunshine. "Well, Ben, how do you feel about your flashback now?" Rusty asked.

"I feel good. I don't have to hate you anymore and feel guilty for it. Grinning, he said, "now I have something else to hate you for: you are going to take my sister away just when she is beginning to bring in some money."

"Ben," Lauren scolded. "He's not taking me away. I'm going to be his wife. It's my choice."

They all discussed the decision Lauren and Cathy had made. Ben said that if it made them happy, he could live with it. And Marie expressed that she was proud of them. "What about you, Mom, have you been saved?" asked Cathy.

"Can't say that I have. We never went to church when I was with your father. I always thought we would some day, but now I don't think I can ever trust God. If He is a good God, why did he let this happen to

Ben, and why did he let my husband walk out on me when I needed him most, and why couldn't I find a decent job instead of having to work in that juke joint, dodging drunks? Why should I believe in Him when He doesn't care about me?"

"Don't say that Mom," Lauren responded.

"Well, I'm happy for you, and I'll go to your baptizing but that's all. I guess you all had better pray for me. We'll see if God hears your prayers."

Later, in private Lauren and Cathy discussed their mother's bitterness and failure to trust God, and decided the best thing they could do was pray for her and demonstrate a Christ like life before her. They believed strongly that God would do His work if they were patient and willing to trust Him.

Meanwhile, Rusty contacted Sarah to see if she could be available to stay with Ben again the next Sunday morning. She was happy to miss church herself to stay with Ben for the special occasion.

At the church, the pastor baptized Lauren and Cathy, and when they had changed clothes they joined Marie and Rusty in the pew. They noticed that both of them had been crying. Pastor Williams brought an inspiring message about living the transformed life in Jesus and challenged Cathy and Lauren and the rest to grow in their faith and commitment.

Chapter 17

TRIAL BY FIRE

Rusty's greatest fear was about to happen. He knew things had been going too well and that Satan was not going to let that go unchallenged.

A new patient, Mrs. Breckenridge, arrived at the nursing home two weeks later. As she was being checked in she reported that a new young doctor in town, Dr. Smythe, was her doctor and that he would be checking on her every week. "He is new so his practice is not so large yet that he can't come here to see me," she said. "He's very handsome," the ninety-year-old added. Lauren got the impression that Mrs. Breckenridge was accustomed to getting what she wanted, and she wanted the special attention of this doctor. "He is as handsome as can be," she repeated. As expected, Dr. Smythe arrived the very next day and demanded that the head nurse accompany him to visit with his patient. He was very handsome, Lauren agreed, when she saw him and heard his British accent, and he is dressed neatly in a blue suit and tie. Sophisticated! Lauren watched carefully as he examined Mrs. Breckenridge with smooth hands. No wonder she likes him, Lauren thought. Then, before she caught herself, she was wondering what it would be like for him to examine her.

Every Tuesday Dr. Smythe came at 11:00 to see his patient and every time he insisted that Lauren accompany him to the room. To be honest, Lauren was glad he did and she began to anticipate his visits and the opportunity to see him, though she felt guilty about it later. After seeing Mrs. Breckenridge he would stop by her office for a chat. "There's nothing wrong with my patient but old age, but I try to humor her by coming anyway, and I get my fee. That also gives me a chance to see you, Lauren." She knew that he must be able to see her blushing at the mere mention of seeing her. "Someday soon I want us to go have lunch together. I'll plan it in my schedule one Tuesday, so keep yours open if possible." Lauren didn't know how to respond, so he said, "goodbye for now," and left hurriedly. Was this more than a professional visit he planned? Didn't he see that engagement ring on her finger? Surely he didn't mean anything more than something professional, she thought. But Lauren couldn't get the dashing young man out of her mind, and found herself daydreaming about him.

The very next Tuesday, Dr. Smythe came and they visited before going to see his patient. "I can't help but notice your British accent. How did you come to be in little Winslow?"

"Yes, I grew up in the city of London then decided to come to the United States to study medicine and just stayed. I came to Winslow because the reports were that a doctor was needed here and I needed to go someplace. So here I am. Let's go see Mrs. Breckenridge and then to lunch." He was so confident that it sounded like their lunch together was already settled.

"I don't know," Lauren tried to protested. "I am engaged to be married soon and the people of the gossipy little town might not understand if they see us together."

"Oh, it will just be a professional luncheon. But if you can spare the time we will drive to the next town where I know of a nice restaurant. In fact, that's what we will do," he said. There is that male dominance again, Lauren thought.

"Can you give me a few minutes?" Lauren asked. She went to the ladies room to freshen up a bit and check her makeup, then informed her staff that she would be gone for a while. She found the good doctor waiting for her at the door where he led her to a fancy little sports car which smacked of money. On their way out of town on Highway 91 they were about to pass Rusty's shop; ashamed, she turned her head so he wouldn't see her if he was looking out. She was thankful that she didn't see him or any of his crew. After a thirty-minute drive Dr. Smythe drove into the parking lot of a fancy lounge/restaurant and hurriedly came around to open the door and take her hand to help her exit the low slung luxury vehicle. The mere touch of his hand made her tingle.

Lauren's host placed the order for his favorite dishes after asking her approval, and he also ordered wine, which Lauren refused. "Dr. Smythe…".

"Call me John please. John Henry Smythe. You know Henry VIII comes in there somewhere. My family is very patriotic British."

"Okay, John. Tell me why you went into medicine?" Lauren suggested to make conversation.

"Well, I come from a long line of medical professionals. My father is a doctor and insisted that I follow in his steps. I think otherwise he might have cut off my allowance and disinherited me. And I did not object to it. After all, it has been a good, lucrative profession for him. It's honorable and it meets a need in every setting. I didn't want to work for the government in social medicine as I would have in England, or get into some fast-paced, demanding location, so I came here."

"And you?" he asked.

"My brother was severely injured several years ago which left him a quadriplegic and I've been very involved in his care, so now I would like to be able to help others."

"That's very noble of you, I must say."

A nice young waitress brought lunch to the table. John thanked her and Lauren noticed that he watched her rear as she walked away and wondered if he watched her the same way. The conversation over lunch was pleasant, and they briefly discussed medical issues and why she chose to work in a nursing home. Then he said, "There are much better places to work where patients will not be so needy." He couldn't seem to understand that she felt called to minister to the most needy. John left a generous tip and paid for the meal with cash and they moved to the car, where again he helped her into the car, elevating her blood pressure she was sure. When he stopped in the front of the nursing home, John reached for her hand and held it while he suggested, "Let's do this again soon. I do so enjoy your company."

"Thank you," she responded without making any promises. She rushed to her office, heady with excitement over what had just happened. "I have to stop feeling this way," she muttered aloud. "I'm afraid I'm being unfaithful to Rusty."

Rusty came by to visit as soon as his work was finished. He was excited that he had found someone to draw the blueprints for their house, but she couldn't share his excitement because again she felt that it was "his" house. He chose the location and was now designing it. "What have you done today, besides work?" he asked.

Lauren felt that she had to be honest with him, so she said, "We have a new doctor in town and he is seeing one of our patients, and he invited me to go to lunch with him today. Since I was tired of the nursing home meals, I accepted."

"Oh, am I supposed to be jealous?" He said with a grin.

"Of course not. It was what he called a 'professional lunch,' and we did discuss some medical issues," she answered, without telling him the whole story. Would he consider that she was unfaithful to him? she wondered. He had been so wonderful to her and her family, and she did love him. Yet, Dr. Smythe is so sophisticated, obviously from a wealthy family, and with experiences in places she had only read about. He was a total contrast to Rusty. "If you ever need to be jealous, I'll let you know," she joked.

In two weeks the house plans were finished and Rusty brought them for her to examine and to make any suggestions for changes. That could have been avoided, she thought, if she had been consulted beforehand. The house Rusty planned was impressive. It would have three bedrooms in the main house; Cathy would have one of them with her own private bath for as long as she needed it. He had planned for an apartment attached to the house where Ben and Marie could live. It would have a specially-designed bathroom to meet Ben's needs, and a separate bathroom adjacent to Marie's bedroom, a living room and a small kitchen. Being a wood worker, Rusty wanted the house to be constructed of wood on a concrete foundation. He had already talked with a contractor with whom he did business to do the construction. The only things left to do were, arrange financing, make whatever changes were needed to the plans, and get it on the contractor's schedule. "And," Rusty announced, "I've already talked with Clark and he has agreed that I can use the business as collateral for the loan; it will be a breeze. And the contractor has also agreed to let me do whatever part of the work I can to save on the cost. And there is one other thing, Lauren, I want us to set a wedding date for about the time the house is complete in about six months. Have you thought about one?"

"Not really, but I'll get on it," she answered.

However, as the weeks passed and construction began, Lauren felt less and less sure about the marriage. Perhaps it was because John Smythe was involving himself in her life more and more, and she was confused about her feelings. "Lord, help me know what to do," she prayed.

Rusty continued pushing her for a wedding date every time he saw her, but she stalled. John was taking her to lunch every Tuesday by then, and they had even gone out together one evening. Since Marie had quit her job, she was at home with Ben in the evening, so Lauren was free. She felt so bad that she wasn't completely honest with Rusty, telling him there was a board of directors' meeting that evening. In truth there was such a meeting, but she was not required to attend. Weeks passed with no firm date for their wedding, and Rusty was so busy working on the house in his spare time that he didn't realize what was happening. Lauren was spending more and more time with John and enjoying it.

Finally, Rusty said, "Lauren, we need to talk. You seem more and more distant, preoccupied. You haven't set a date yet and the house will be finished soon. What's wrong? Are you having second thoughts?"

"Rusty," she began, "I care deeply for you, and I appreciate so much all you have done for us, but I'm just not quite ready. I think I ought to be more certain before I make a lifetime commitment. I think I just need more time. Could you wait a little longer? Maybe if we just spent a little time apart I could get more secure in my decision. Please understand."

Rusty was shocked, not angry, but hurt. He couldn't bear the thought of life without Lauren in it. "What is behind this? Oh, you have been talking a lot about this doctor what's his name, John? Are you getting involved with him and ditching me? I just can't believe it. I love you with all of my heart, Lauren, and I thought you loved me too. Well, I want you to know that I'm not giving up. I'll do whatever I need to. What can I do?"

"I don't know," Rusty. "I can't stand for you to be mad at me, but, yes, I have grown close to John Smythe and I am very fond of him. I don't love him, but I'm attracted to him, even though I never wanted this to happen. I'm just asking for a little more time to sort this out. Let me give you this ring and car keys back until I'm settled."

"No, Lauren. I'll hold the ring until I can place it on your finger again for life, but you need the car for transportation, and I don't need it now, so you keep the keys and use the car. I'm going to work on the house now, but I'll still be seeing you, Lauren." And he did: he still talked with her at the nursing home on Thursdays and sat beside her in church, taking her hand and holding it during the service. And he also continued to visit Marie and Ben and help them in any way possible.

On one of his visits to the Appleby home, Rusty felt led to talk with Marie and Ben about the Lord. He expected rejection, but soon discovered that Marie had been thinking about her need for the Lord, so in Ben's presence Rusty shared the scriptures with her and asked her if she would pray for salvation. She was ready and when she finished, Ben said, "me too." Right there Rusty rejoiced and thanked the Lord and made plans to get both of them to church Sunday. It wouldn't be easy, but he still had the ramp and he would find a way to make it happen. The next day, Rusty consulted with the pastor and learned they would need a little ramp constructed, so he set to work to build it and have it ready.

Sunday morning, after Lauren and Cathy had left to go to Sunday school, Rusty drove out to help Marie and Ben get to church. He had found out that they had not told Lauren and Cathy because Ben wanted to keep it a secret and surprise them. They arrived at the church just at the beginning of the worship service, and Ben rolled into the church and forward to a spot specially designed for wheel chairs. Rusty could see that Lauren and Cathy could hardly believe what they were seeing, but they moved to sit near Mom, Ben, and Rusty. When the invitation was given Ben moved his chair forward, with Marie holding on to it, and they made their professions of faith. After the service, Cathy beamed, "We are a family twice, once by blood and again by spirit." After the service, Lauren stopped to get them boxed lunches while Rusty went to get Ben into the house. Lunch was a happy occasion for everyone, even though Rusty was reserved. Marie and Cathy noticed the coolness between him and Lauren and that the ring was missing, but they said nothing about it at the time.

Shortly after lunch, Rusty excused himself, and Marie asked what was going on. "Things are on hold for now," Lauren said.

"Does that mean you and Rusty may not get married?"

"I don't want to talk about it now," Mom.

For the next three weeks Rusty stayed busy working on the house, and Lauren spent more and more time with Dr. Smythe. Wanting to know him better, one evening, since she had never heard him make any reference to God or church, she asked him where he went to church.

"I don't go to church," he responded. I don't need it. Science has all the answers and power I need. And as for the Bible I believe it's a lot of myth that some overactive imagination came up with."

Lauren was shocked but made no reply, wondering if there was any way she could ever change his mind; however, she was troubled by his beliefs. Still she enjoyed his good disposition and company and didn't want to lose him. Later as they shared the loveseat in his apartment, they became involved in some passionate kissing. She feared it was going too far. Then he rose from the couch, took her hand and started leading her toward the bedroom. It was then that she drew the first line. "No," she said emphatically. "I can't do that."

Frustrated, the good doctor proceeded to persuade her. "Ah, come on Lauren. Listen," he said, "your old fashioned morality is just too out of date. Don't you know that love making is a natural thing. Look at the animal world; they have no inhibitions. That Bible believing has just convinced you that some good things are evil. If you let it, that will warp your mind. We are adults and free to do whatever we want as long as we are not harming others."

"But I think it would harm me," Lauren protested.

"How? I'm not going to hurt you. It will be pleasurable and satisfying. You'll see."

"No," Lauren refused. "I think it will harm me emotionally and spiritually, if not physically. I think I had better go for tonight." The next morning a dozen red rose were delivered to her office, and Lauren thought maybe she had just overreacted the night before. For the rest of the day she did her best to push it out of her mind as something that probably happens in every relationship as it develops.

Lauren found herself making a list of comparisons between Rusty and John. Rusty was a common, hard-working businessman: John was a sophisticated, well-educated medical doctor. Rusty was a stay-at-home guy: John was a world traveler. Rusty would always wear work clothes; John dressed in fine attire. But Rusty was loyal: John seemed to have a roving eye. Rusty had faith in God: John had faith in science: Rusty cared for her family and others: John cared about himself. Looking at her list, Lauren realized that the choice should be easy, yet she couldn't tear herself away from John.

Tuesday Dr. Smythe came in his usual chipper mood and stopped by Lauren's office first for his usual cordial visit. Nothing was mentioned about their previous experience. Then he spoke, "Well, let's go down to see the old Breckenridge witch."

"John, what do you mean?" Lauren demanded. "Don't you love your patients?"

"Look, I'm a medical professional. My job is to see patients and treat illnesses. Beyond that I have no responsibility for them. I don't have to care about them or love them. When I've done my duty to them, I'm through. The practice of medicine must be objective, depending on science, not emotion."

"Oh, that's so different from what I've been taught. Maybe that's the difference between the doctor who prescribes treatment and the nurse who administers it," she muttered.

"Well, you do it your way, and I'll do it mine," John replied.

After seeing Mrs. Breckenridge, as he was leaving, Dr. Smythe said to Lauren, "I'm going to cook dinner for us this evening. I would like to discuss something very important with you. Will you come?"

"Just discuss?"

"Yes."

"Then I'll be there."

That evening Lauren and John enjoyed a delicious meal of flounder, vegetables, and tapioca pudding for dessert. As usual, Lauren declined the wine he offered. Then soon after they had cleared the table and put the dishes in the dishwasher, they went to sit in the living area. "Lauren," John began," I have a serious proposal to make to you."

"Oh, really? The most serious proposal I know is for marriage," Lauren laughed.

"Well, it's not quite that yet," John confessed. "I would like for you to move in with me and for us to live together. Everybody is doing it these days. Marriage is such a demanding commitment and shouldn't be entered into lightly, but after we've tested our love together, then in a year or two, if we choose to we can marry."

Lauren hadn't seen that coming. For her, courtship always led to marriage, then the enjoyment of intimacy. So she said, "I'm sorry, John, but I am afraid I can't accept."

"Why not?" He queried. "Is it that restraining biblical morality again?"

"Yes, it is my convictions. It's the way I have always been taught and accepted as proper. And, yes, it's against what the Bible teaches. Besides I can't move out of the house because of Ben's needs. I can't just abandon Mom."

"Look," John continued, "you are not responsible for them. You can't go on being their provider. In fact, I've considered that and I think I have an ideal solution."

"Oh? Then you've really thought about this?" she asked.

"I know this facility that treats nothing but paralyzed, long-term patients. All of the patients suffer from the same kind of problems and they get the best of care. The cost is only about twice that of a traditional nursing home but if you contribute part of that, your mother can go back to work to pay the balance. You would be free of any responsibility for Ben, and you could even go to see him every year. How does that sound?"

"Where is this facility?" she asked.

"It's in a beautiful setting in upstate New York."

Lauren couldn't believe what she was hearing and suddenly realized the mistake she had made. Angrily, she said, "John, I'll tell you what I believe. You are an insensitive, uncaring, self-centered, pompous jerk."

"What are you talking about?" he asked.

"You don't believe in God or His Word; you don't believe in church; you don't care anything for your patients except for their money; and you are unconcerned about my convictions and my family. I've finally realized that you don't fit in my life at all. Thank you for dinner. Now I'm going home to help with Ben, and I don't want to ever see you again. I'll assign someone to go with you to see your patient on Tuesdays. Goodnight." With John looking baffled, she grabbed her purse and slammed the door as she left.

Lauren sat in the car Rusty had bought and allowed her to use and cried. What had she done to Rusty? Would he ever forgive her? she wondered. Finally she was able to clear her teary eyes enough to drive home, wondering how she could ever face Rusty again.

For the rest of the week, Lauren made it a point not to see Rusty or John. To herself and to God she confessed her waywardness, and sought

God's forgiveness as she would have to seek Rusty's. Sunday morning came and Cathy stayed with Ben so Marie could go to church with Lauren. Sitting in their usual place, Rusty came and sat beside Lauren and reached for her hand, and as he squeezed her hand she squeezed his in return.

The pastor announced that the message was his once-a-year sermon when he spoke to the young about choosing a mate. Lauren could hardly believe it; had God sent the message for her? She listened carefully and made notes as the pastor said, "God has a mate for you already picked out. It's your job through prayer and obedience to discover His choice for you. Be sure to marry the person you love more than you love yourself and the one who loves you equally. Marry someone who shares your faith and values so you will not be unequally yoked together. Marry someone who will be true and loyal to you throughout life. Marry someone you can look at every morning, with hair mused, without makeup, unshaven and with morning breath, and say "Thank you, Lord, for this mate you've sent me." As the sermon came to a close, Lauren leaned over and whispered to Rusty, "If you will still have me, I'll be your mate forever." Rusty became so excited that he could hardly contain himself until after the closing prayer. Then he jumped to his feet and shouted, "Folks, we're getting married, and you're all invited to the wedding."

Marie drove Lauren's car home to allow the couple to lunch together and then to go see the almost completed house. "Rusty, I can't believe the wonderful job you have done in selecting everything for this house from the site to the paint. I do have a confession to make, though. When you made major decisions about it without considering my opinion, I was hurt. I know I couldn't have done a better job, and I would have agreed with you on every one of them, but it was just the feeling of being left out that hurt so much."

"Lauren, I am so sorry I was so insensitive," Rusty apologized. I guess I was more interested in surprising you than consulting you. I promise you that if you will forgive me, it won't happen again."

Lauren led Rusty to sit on a workbench and said, "Rusty, I am the one who needs your forgiveness. I was fascinated with a man whose life, experience, demeanor, wealth, and sophistication were so different from my whole life that I got lost to all reason and God's will for me. Can you ever forgive me? I promise I know where I belong now."

"Absolutely," Rusty responded, planting a passionate kiss on her lips. I never doubted that you would become my wife. I just felt that you were like Moses and the Israelites, that you had to wander in the wilderness before you came home. With that, he reached in his pocket and pulled out the box containing her engagement ring. He explained that the box was worn because he had carried it in his pocket every day waiting for the day when he could slip the ring on her finger again. She cried as he did it, and he kissed away the tears. "Now let's make some wedding plans," he said. "I'm not making them without you, but let me tell you what I've dreamed of. The house will be finished in two weeks. If we can both take a week off work, we'll enjoy a honeymoon anywhere you wish then move into the house and bring your family in it also. It will become home then."

"Rusty do you think we could spend our honeymoon right here in our new house? That's what I would like; then we can move our family in."

That sounded good to Rusty so they decided to marry without a lot of fanfare in two weeks. They honored Lauren's wish to ask Cathy to be the maid of honor and Clark to be the best man. Since Lauren was not sure she could ask or expect her father to give her in marriage, Rusty suggested, "I have an idea. Let's ask Ben to escort you down the aisle with his chair and give you away."

"That's a wonderful idea, Rusty. I like it, and Ben will be so excited. Do you think there will be room for me to walk beside him in the aisle?"

"I think so."

Like a bride, Lauren worried, "That's so soon and we will have so much to get done in a hurry. We may not have time to get invitations and get them mailed. Then there is the reception."

"Lauren, the people we will want to invite are here at church, at my workplace and yours. Why don't we just announce it in each place and invite them to come? And we can get the reception catered. Uh oh, here I go again, trying to make the plans."

"No. I like the idea. Let's do that."

Two weeks later, they watched Ben, dressed in a tuxedo, wheel his chair down the aisle with beautiful Lauren holding onto his arm, to meet Rusty at the altar. When the "I do's" were said and the pastor prayed for God's blessings on their marriage, they moved to the reception room to receive the guests and hear their congratulations and best wishes. Lauren whispered to Marie as she came through the line, "start packing." As they moved toward the well-decorated car, some shouted, "Where are you going for a honeymoon."

> In unison the bride and groom answered "Home."
> "There is a river that washes you clean
> There is a tree that marks the places you've been
> Blood that was spilled, although not your own
>
> For all of your tears
> Are the wages for things you've done
> And all of those nights
> Spent alone in the darkness of your mind
>
> Give it up
> These are the things
> You were never meant to shoulder."
>
> --Lyrics from "There is a River"
> by Jars of Clay

Epilogue

After the honeymoon, Marie and Ben were moved into their apartment and Cathy, who was near the end of her physical therapy training took over the guest bedroom. She went on to graduate and begin a practice in Winslow. Then she fell in love with a young engineer who had been one of her patients after his motorcycle accident, and they married and settled in Winslow. Marie was provided an allowance and she stayed with Ben and cooked the meals for the entire family and they ate together as a family.

Lauren and Rusty purchased the TLC Nursing Home where she began making changes that made it the favored nursing home in town and she soon had a waiting list of people who wanted to move in. She continued to be the head nurse and maintain personal contact with the patients.

Unfortunately, two years later Ben was diagnosed with widespread bone cancer and lived only a few weeks. Marie found herself free, but it was a good thing for Lauren and Rusty's firstborn was expected in a few weeks, and Marie so wanted to be the nanny for this one and others that would follow.

Rusty expanded Clark's Woodworking to supply molding to building supply stores around the state.

Personal

Robert lives, along with his wife Evelyn, on a few acres in rural North Louisiana. Their fifty-five years of marriage have been blessed with four children and their families. Through the years he has earned a B.A. with a major in religion from Louisiana [Baptist] College, an M.A. in English from the University of Louisiana at Monroe, a Master of Divinity and Doctor of Ministry from Luther Rice Seminary. In addition, he has done further studies at Louisiana State University. For most of his adult life Holloway has been a pastor of Baptist churches, and until his retirement, he also taught for twenty-three of those years in the English Department of the University of Louisiana at Monroe. He continues to serve as pastor of the Watson Baptist Church of West Monroe, Louisiana.